Eva Gill lives in South Africa with her husband and her pet bunnies, tarantulas and dogs. She writes full time when she isn't tying up beautiful little submissives whilst listening to classical music, preferably Mozart. Her friends and family mean the world to her, as does the support of her local BDSM community.

The subject matter in her novels is very much a part of her life, where BDSM and normality blur into happy harmony. She loves tattoos, on herself as well as on others. *The Gifts of the Masters* is her third full-length novel, and there are many more to come.

Follow her on Instagram @authorevagill to keep up with her sexy escapades!

Eva Gill

Chimera

CHIMERA PAPERBACK

© Copyright 2018
Eva Gill

The right of Eva Gill to be identified as author of
this work has been asserted by her in accordance with the
Copyright, Designs and Patents Act 1988.

All Rights Reserved

No reproduction, copy or transmission of this publication
may be made without written permission.
No paragraph of this publication may be reproduced,
copied or transmitted save with the written permission or in accordance
with the provisions
of the Copyright Act 1956 (as amended).

Any person who commits any unauthorised act in relation to
this publication may be liable to criminal
prosecution and civil claims for damages.

A CIP catalogue record for this title is
available from the British Library.

ISBN 978 1 903136 60 7

Chimera is an imprint of
Pegasus Elliot MacKenzie Publishers Ltd.
www.pegasuspublishers.com

First Published in 2018

Chimera
**Sheraton House Castle Park
Cambridge England**

Printed & Bound in Great Britain

Acknowledgments

I have many people to thank for their never ending support in this work. My husband, thank you for holding my hand and telling me I am not crap, because writers need those words… (I think we are all needy like that). To Samantha, you rock, you radiate so much love into the world, and I would go mad if I couldn't see you or talk to you (and your bunnies). I love you! My family, the Gills, I love you. Thank you for supporting me, even though at times you must think I am completely bonkers. To Ginger, yes, I am calling you that here! Thanks for some serious character inspiration, late night chats when I couldn't sleep, and some seriously dodgy conversation about seriously dodgy topics. Dude, you are the brother I need, love you! Oh, and the proofreaders, thank you for reading first drafts without complaints.

Thank you to Pegasus Elliot Mackenzie Publishers; you have been amazing and a team beyond comparison.

Part One

Chapter 1

Jonah MacPherson walked from his office to the coffee cart on the sidewalk, rubbing his temples in exhaustion. He ordered his standard decaf cappuccino, exactly as he did every evening when he left the office. It was five-thirty on a Friday afternoon and he was quietly dreading the weekend. He had plans to meet Kevin, a high school friend who happened to be in town, for a beer and dinner at his local bar, the BistroRX, perhaps with a few other friends. Then, an early evening at home.

He hopped on the tram, enjoying the scenery on the way to his apartment in Patterson Park. It was a fairly new district in Baltimore and the hub of the younger, and more hip, business crowd. The block he owned an apartment in gleamed, shiny with glass and chrome, the perfect bachelor's pad. Most of the tenants were forty or under and childless; it suited him.

Jonah dropped his laptop bag on the light-wood chair at his door and walked straight to the bathroom. He stripped off and stood under the steamy spray of the shower, lathering shampoo through his short black hair, and scrubbed his body down with the fresh-scented body wash. He felt the stiffness in his shoulders from the gym the day before, and stretched his arms overhead. He always got sore after he was paired with Blaine in their Mixed Martial Arts classes.

After he towelled off with one of the dark grey towels he pulled from the shelf, he slid open the mirrored door and stood staring into his closet. He chose a simple pair of black chinos and a button-down black shirt, rolling the sleeves back to just below his elbows and leaving the top button undone. The dark colours always worked well.

Barely thirty minutes later, he walked into the BistroRX two blocks away. Jonah could feel gazes shift toward him as Kevin called his name from a table near the back: "Jonah! Hey, come join me."

With his hands in his pockets, he strolled through the tables and past the press of bodies at the bar, almost stopped in his tracks by a particularly intense look directed at him by a young brunette. She turned when he bumped her lightly in the throng of people.

"I'm sorry, excuse me," he said, politely placing a hand on her arm. The electric shock through his fingers, from the contact with her skin, startled him, and clearly startled her, too. Jonah jerked his hand away. He stared for a while longer but the moment was gone. She returned to her conversation, and he walked on toward Kevin.

Kevin gripped his hand in a firm shake, passed him a beer and they sat back to catch up on the week's happenings, relaxing on the leather couches. Nobody else out of their group of five or so friends had pitched up, making excuses like 'family, tired after a long week,' etc.

The vibe in BistroRX became more upbeat as the evening wore on, and an hour later two girls approached them, sashaying along, hips moving seductively.

Jonah's gaze met a pair of startling sea green eyes framed by long dark lashes, held in a face showing a sexy, yet somehow innocent, smile.

"Hey, would you guys care to buy two girls a drink?" she purred, her voice husky and sensual as she brushed her long glossy hair over her shoulder.

Jonah stood, speechless. It was the girl from the bar, and there was something about her that left him spellbound and incapable of forming words.

"I, uh, um," he stuttered, frustrated, because this never happened.

Kevin came to his rescue, leaning forward. He put on a mock-aristocratic air as he spoke. "Please excuse my friend here, he tends to lose his voice around pretty girls. We would gladly do so, should the ladies in question care to divulge their names?" His eyebrow raised, his usual cocky attitude in place.

Dark-hair shook her head, making that lovely hair swish behind her, over her shoulder. She smiled. "I am Anya and this is my friend Laila." She gestured to the statuesque blonde at her side.

Jonah reached out to shake their hands, and again the electricity between his hand and Anya's was there. She met his gaze, and her smile disappeared. "You felt that, right, it's not just me?" she whispered, so that only he could hear.

He swallowed and nodded. They separated and he greeted Laila similarly, but she kept her eyes down and her demeanour was shy and reserved. The girls joined them in their corner, and three of them chatted genially, making the requisite small talk about jobs and hobbies, while Laila sat shyly at Anya's side. At eleven, Anya looked down at her watch, and she and Laila exchanged a loaded glance, one that was not missed by the men.

Anya stood and pulled Jonah aside. "We must go, but I would very much like to see you again, soon." Her breath felt surprisingly cool in his neck, and she leaned close so that Kevin could not hear her speak. "I do not trust your friend, but if you are brave and wish to follow the chemistry between us, and you want your life to change, come to this address after midnight tonight. I will make sure the doorman is expecting you."

Jonah felt her press a card into his hand.

With a deep breath, he nodded. "I'll come. I just need to shake him off. I don't think that will be a problem, though."

Laila had moved to wait by the door, and Kevin was already making his move toward a redhead at the bar.

Anya vanished and Jonah exhaled loudly, questioning his own sanity. He never did things impulsively. He caught Kevin's attention and tapped his watch, gesturing toward the door. The other man waved and pointed at the redhead, a crude leer on his face. Jonah frowned, shaking his head, and walked out. Only once he was through the door did he look at the business card.

It was exquisite, cream linen paper and had an address on West Arlington Street written on it, below the image of a chalice. He frowned; that was not the best part of town to be heading to, especially at this time of night. He had to do it though, so he pulled out his mobile and dialled a yellow cab service. How would a stranger know anything about his life? Why would she think he'd want to change it?

***

The cab driver looked a little concerned when Jonah read off the address.

"You sure about that, Mr?" he asked, glancing up and down at Jonah's attire.

"Yeah I am sure." The words were confident but the tone certainly didn't convey the sentiment. Jonah stepped out of the cab at the given street number. It was nothing but a derelict mansion on the corner.

He slowly walked closer, completely on guard. When the front door opened smoothly and dim light shone through the crack, a man in a black suit approached Jonah.

He stopped two steps away. "Good evening sir, are you the guest of the slave Anya?"

Jonah nodded carefully, and the man led him through the door by the elbow.

"Come inside please, sir, we do not like to be seen at this entrance, someone may notice."

Jonah stood in a small foyer and frowned as the man took his coat from him. In the chilly air outside he had donned his favourite, heavy black Melton coat, bought at Zara on a past trip to London. He couldn't help but think the man reminded him of the elegant older butlers you sometimes saw in movies.

The item of clothing was tenderly hung on a hanger and placed on a rail against the wall; it was uncanny to see such respect paid to a piece of material. Jonah frowned. Why would he notice how his jacket was being treated in the midst of such mystery? He chuckled. It was nerves. He paid attention to random details when he got nervous. The man had called Anya a slave, but why? Who did she serve? And 'slave' in this day and age, really? What had he just walked into?

He stared at the décor, in complete contrast to the outside of the ramshackle and abandoned-looking building. It was merely an entrance room, the gateway to something bigger. The walls seemed alive with the black, damask velvet detailed papering, or paint, he could not tell which it was. The light fittings were ornate medieval brass artworks fitted into sconces just above head-height, on each of the four walls. He ran his shoe over the plush carpeting, a purple so dark it might have been blue, perhaps even black.

Jonah could hear music beyond a carved and intricately detailed dark wood double-door, set with an arched top. His heart raced when the black-suited man walked toward those doors.

He turned briefly to face Jonah. "Please wait here sir, I will call the slave Anya to come and fetch you. An uninitiated one is not permitted beyond this door unaccompanied."

Without bothering to explain any of the terms he had just used, he disappeared through the door.

The 'slave'. Jonah mused again at the word. 'Uninitiated'... what did it all mean? His questions would be answered when he saw Anya, he knew this, but he felt very confused. What was this place?

***

After ten minutes, when he was still alone, he took a seat on a deep purple couch. The velvety fabric resembled the colour of bruised eggplant, he thought, frowning. He was still stroking the soft material absentmindedly when the inner door opened and the suited man walked through, followed by Anya. Except that it wasn't the same Anya. Everything about this woman was different.

Jonah almost didn't recognise her, as she was stark naked under a sheer, deep purple, chiffon garment. She wore an intricate gold collar around her neck, and similar cuffs at her wrists, and left *nothing* to his imagination. Her hair was gathered in a high ponytail on top of her head, revealing amazing bone structure and almond-shaped, slightly slanted, emerald green eyes. Yes, he had been mistaken about their colour earlier, they were definitely emerald green and not sea green. All traces of makeup had been cleaned from her face and her skin glowed, healthy and clear.

"Hello Jonah. I am glad you came," she said, her voice soft. She bowed low, revealing a small padlock at the rear of the collar as she lowered her head and stretched her arms out, the garment forming gossamer wings. She raised her eyes to him demurely, from her gracefully bent position. "Follow me."

Jonah started speaking and reached for her, but she quickly stepped out of his reach.

"Don't touch me!" she hissed, and then lowered her voice to a whisper. "Not here. Come inside with me and I will explain the rules and answer any questions you may have, that I am allowed to."

Anya turned from him, pushed open the double doors and walked through.

The sight before him was unlike any scene Jonah had ever imagined. He followed Anya to a table. When she beckoned him to sit, he fell into an armchair automatically.

"Can I get you a drink?" Anya's voice was soft, at ear level.

"Single-malt scotch, please," Jonah murmured, his eyes fixed on a young woman tied to a cross in a central, sunken floor space below. A tall man dressed in long, dark, hooded robes stood over her with a multi-stranded instrument that looked like a whip of some sort. At present, he was running his hand down her flanks, and Jonah saw her head fall back against the man's shoulder, her eyes closed.

At the girl's neck and wrists sat the same gold collar and cuffs that Anya wore, and her glossy, pale white hair was in the same ponytail. Jonah frowned when the big man stepped away from her. It was Laila, the other girl from the club. For a moment he swore the man was Blaine, his MMA training partner. He brushed the notion aside, although as he watched the man move he was more and more convinced. The hood hid his face, though.

When the whip flew through the air and made contact with pale skin, Jonah had to stifle his scream and shove his fist into his mouth. He could not believe what he was seeing. The woman jerked on her restraints, her hands visibly tightening on the cuffs at her wrists, but her moan was not one of pain. She breathed harder as the blows fell. He watched her ribcage rise and fall, and when the blows ended, Jonah could see her shoulders heaving. The robed man placed his whip on a counter and moved to stand behind her. The robe concealed most of his movements, but Jonah saw the woman lean her lower body toward him, and moments later, the man's head was at her neck, his arm around the front of her body. Jonah heard her cries as she came, even over the music. The sound of pleasure was so distinct, so unmistakeable that it aroused him, and he shifted in his seat, adjusting his pants to accommodate the swell of his erection.

Jonah was mesmerized by what he was watching. The woman was being gently untied when Anya knelt to place his drink next to him. She also handed him a white cloak.

"Are you serious? I have to wear this?" He stared at her, amused.

Her face was serious as she nodded. "Yes, it shows that you are uninitiated. People are not to approach you without being aware of this." She smiled at his clothes. "Not that they wouldn't know, but trust me, you want it, even if you are just sitting here."

Jonah thought it best to take her advice on this, and stood to swing the cloak around his shoulders.

When he sat back down, she had sunk back into her graceful kneeling position on the floor, and was looking earnestly up at him.

"You must have questions? I'm so sorry. I could not tell you more without showing you."

Jonah picked up his scotch. "I have so many. It might take you getting the ball rolling though, because I don't even know what I am looking at."

Anya giggled quietly, "A true vanilla then." and they both looked up as a couple walked past, a girl clad similarly to Anya, on a leash, following a cloaked man. When Jonah looked at Anya's face, her expression was one of total respect and reverence.

Jonah raised an eyebrow, and out of the pure absurdity of the situation, chuckled. "Okay, naked one, tell me what you've walked me into."

Anya spoke softly. "I brought you here because I saw something in your eyes tonight, in the single instant our eyes met. I saw all the boredom, disillusionment, and your feelings of being trapped in the mundane. I saw a little of me, of how I felt when I came to this life many years ago. Tell me I'm wrong?"

He looked down at her in total disbelief. "Carry on," he murmured.

"This place, Jonah, I cannot even tell you its name. You cannot enter and would never have found it without an invite from one who belongs, like me. I found my way here through another, who saw similar attributes in me many years ago. I have never been happier, or more fulfilled."

Jonah stopped her. "So what exactly is this place you can't tell me the name of? Pardon me if I'm sceptical…"

She smiled mysteriously. "It is a very exclusive BDSM club, where people come to learn and enjoy their private desires and taboo fantasies. They either find their inner devoted slave, such as myself, or they learn how to become a Master or Mistress to a slave or submissive. They are introduced to such a mate, and there's more, but that I cannot share. A Master has to condone the sharing of the sacred knowledge."

Jonah's eyes widened. "Oh God, it's a sex club."

Anya rolled her eyes, and a fire flared in her. "You ignorant fool. BDSM is not all about sex, and that is one of the first things people who come here learn. The Forgotten Realm has a set of rules, and a ritual-based system that everything works by. It's called 'protocol' here. Slaves and submissives respect the Masters and Mistresses. They own us while we are on this property, by our consent, and respect our individual owners' rights to us. I am not going to tell you more tonight, do some research about the basics, Google is a wonderful tool…"

Jonah had finished his whiskey. It felt as though hours had passed during which he had learned too much.

Another suited man, older, perhaps in his sixties, approached Jonah and Anya, holding Jonah's coat and an envelope with Jonah's name on it. He passed them to Jonah.

"For you, sir, from the Masters. Slave Anya is to show you out now. A taxi is waiting to take you home, it is paid for by us. Have a good night." He bowed before he turned to leave.

Anya led Jonah to the door, her gait the smoothest, most graceful walk he had ever seen on a woman, the gossamer fabric flowing behind her. There was something surreal about her movements, and the diaphanous fabric shimmered as she walked. At the door she bowed to him, and with a darkly sensual glance said, "I sincerely hope that I see you again, Jonah MacPherson, there is so much we can give you, so much I could give you..." With a last glance of those green eyes she shut the door and he was left on the sidewalk in the cold.

His taxi honked, and Jonah slid into the cold leather seat. As it pulled away, he exhaled hard and rubbed his temples, staring at the envelope in his lap in shock. He had never told Anya his surname was MacPherson...

***

At home, Jonah paced his living room. He held the envelope in his hands, still too nervous to open it. He wished he knew how they had come by his surname, and so quickly. He put the card down on his couch, upright against a pillow, and walked over to his built in bar to pour a scotch, watching the smooth, twelve year old Glenfiddich flow into the crystal glass.

He sat down next to the foreboding envelope, and with a deep breath, slipped his finger under the elaborate wax seal, which was, of course, deep purple and embedded with the symbol of a chalice. When he unfolded the card inside, he had to blink a few times.

Dear Mr. MacPherson,

We apologise for all the mystery, but it is better this way, should your final answer be no. My name is of no importance as yet, but how we know yours is troubling to you I am sure.
If this, as well as what you got a glimpse of tonight, intrigues you, meet me at the Manhattan on Tuesday for lunch, 14:00, be prompt.
I will know you by sight.

It was unsigned, and he dropped it on his coffee table as though it were a snake. Jonah was suddenly overcome with exhaustion; it was half past three on a Saturday morning and he desperately needed to get some rest. With his head still spinning and his mind full of disturbing images, he fell into a restless sleep.

When he woke the next morning, he turned off his cellular. He didn't feel like speaking to anybody and had some research to do. While he stood in front of his coffee machine watching the rich, dark liquid drip into the glass jug, his nose filled with the scent of the Italian grind, he replayed the image of Laila tied to the cross, being whipped by the tall, cloaked figure. He was so distracted by his musing over whether the man could have been Blaine that he overfilled his mug when he poured in the milk. Strong dark coffee went flowing over the counter.

"Fuck!" Jonah cursed, grabbing a dish towel and wiping up the spill.

He took the coffee to his study and sat down behind his computer, swiping his fingers over the mousepad to activate the screen. When it came to life, he clicked on Internet Explorer. He thought for a few seconds, and then researched the word 'dominance'. The sites and images that popped up were arousing beyond belief. He read through what he found under searches for 'slave', 'BDSM' and 'submissive'. Jonah sat back in his chair, running his fingers through his hair. He had a hard-on so intense he could not think; he rubbed gingerly over the granite of his cock in his jeans. At least the research had helped him come to one decision: he certainly did not see himself as submissive, no way, no how.

Jonah didn't even realize how much of the day had passed while he sat mesmerized behind his computer. His eyes burned when he finally looked away and stared out through the window, at the setting sun. His stomach growled and he realized he hadn't eaten.

***

The apartment Jonah lived in was his own personal haven. From the outside, it was cold, steel and glass. Inside, though, he had made it comfortable. The floors throughout were a laminate wood, and a warm red rug marked his lounge. His couch was of a soft cream fabric, and the scatter cushions were in bold reds and browns. When he poured a glass of wine and strolled down the passage to his bedroom he stared at the large bed, and the first thought he had was of Olivia, lying curled in it with her glasses perched on her nose, a book in her hands.

If he had to think about it, this apartment perhaps held too many memories of her. They had met at Kevin's wedding, fallen into bed after the reception, and never surfaced from a convenient situation. He'd asked her to move in, they'd lived together for two years, and then things had gone wrong when she realised she wasn't going to be Mrs. MacPherson. He had started feeling trapped, as though he should propose, but couldn't. How do you commit to someone for an eternity when you can't picture your future, and having children, with them?

He never felt the electrifying chemistry with her, that he'd experienced the first time he had touched Anya. Perhaps he'd secretly known he needed more. More than sweet smiles and Sunday breakfasts in bed, more than the mundane existence they had lived in, unplanned.

When Olivia had moved out, realising things were not going her way, it had left Jonah a bit broken for having hurt her, yet also quite relieved. It made him rethink his life thoroughly, but never would he have had the thoughts he was now having. BDSM? A club he didn't know the name of, in a derelict old building? A slave girl called Anya, with the most captivating green eyes…

Jonah had no idea what lay ahead for him, and he was excited. It was a feeling he had not experienced in years. His heart beat a little faster and he felt more alive. While he stood there surveying his bedroom, and had flashbacks to all the times he had spent there with Olivia, the comfortable love and the fights about the future, and in the end the indifference that had killed their bond, he thought of selling the place.

No decision made in haste is ever a good one, he said to himself as he walked out, brushing aside the thought.

***

Jonah's career was demanding, and in his office environment he was a consummate professional. The accounting firm he worked for catered to large, corporate clients, and had a small auditing department. They audited businesses to assess their compliance to the IRS tax laws, to make sure they paid their dues.

His parents had nurtured his intellect and pushed him to work hard and achieve a degree, and because he had a very mathematical brain, Jonah had flourished in accounting, managing to gain a position as an auditor, which was considered fairly elite. He worked from eight to five every day, and was still looking for something to do over the weekends that would remind him what it felt like to live again. Currently, he was an automaton, a robot. He woke up, had his coffee, worked, went to gym, worked, had a cappuccino, and went home. On a Friday he sometimes met Kevin for drinks, and the rest of his weekend was filled with trivial activity, family visits and being alone.

He had lost Olivia and had not dated since. Now, all he could think about was Anya. Anya and that diaphanous garment she wore last night. He thought of her collarbones, her beautiful and flawless skin. Jonah pictured her breasts, small and perky, the nipples rose-coloured. He had seen everything in the dim light. There had been not a hair on her sex, and from his guess, neither had there been any on the rest of her body. Her legs were long and slender, and she had the look of a woman who went to gym and took care of herself.

The rest of the weekend passed without event, and on Monday he performed his standard routine of preparing for work, dressing, having coffee and toast, and skipping down the stairs to reach the lobby. The only problem was that he was more conscious of his mental boredom, his lack of joy in life, and his yearning for more, for love. He walked the block to catch a tram and jumped on the correct one, all the while cursing Anya for awakening this awareness in him.

Monday soon passed, and so did Tuesday morning. When Jonah stepped through the door of the Manhattan Hotel's restaurant on Tuesday afternoon, his heart thundered in his throat and a cold sweat broke out across his forehead. A small part of him prayed it would be Anya there, but he knew better, and took a seat at the bar to order a gin and tonic.

He had taken the afternoon off to go home and post his apartment for sale, and the agent was coming over at five. The hasty late-night idea had turned into a carefully thought out decision. It was time to move on from Olivia, and everything that constantly reminded him of her.

When a man in his sixties sat down at the bar on the stool next to Jonah, he looked up briefly and smiled, then looked back down and disappeared into his own thoughts.

The man spoke, in a very cultured British accent. "I'm so glad you decided to come, Jonah. Good afternoon."

Chapter 2

Jonah turned slowly toward him. "Hi." He was at a loss as to how to respond. "I'm not really sure what I'm supposed to say, so pardon me if I let you do most of the talking." He felt as though he had lost all self-assurance in the presence of this man, who exuded calm the way normal humans excreted sweat.

With a chuckle, the other man beckoned over a bartender. "My name is Bartholomew Black," he said to Jonah, and then ordered a glass of red wine. "Shall we sit at a table? It might provide more privacy for discussing delicate topics." He glanced at the patrons close-by.

They moved to a booth, where Jonah sank down into the red velvet padded bench, quietly wondering to himself, once again, what the hell he was doing.

With little lines of concentration between his eyes, Bartholomew answered Jonah's unspoken question. "I'll tell you what you are doing, Mr. MacPherson. You are bored with your life. Why, just this past weekend you were reminiscing about a past relationship, now you are on the verge of selling your apartment. You are lonely, and you cannot stop, for even one moment, thinking of Anya. What you saw and where she took you occupies your every waking thought. And now that I have brought her up, and what you saw, you are aroused…"

"Stop!" Jonah exclaimed. "How do you… what… you… can you…" He stammered and fell over the words he could not articulate. He stared open-mouthed at the strange man who sat opposite him, and took a good look at Bartholomew. His eyes. That's what gave away that he was different. Jonah shook his head. Surely this was not possible. He blinked and then looked again. Normal. "But I thought I saw…"

"Sometimes we should believe what we initially see and follow our gut, Mr. MacPherson. But we repress our animal instincts. The world has killed our ability to listen to gut feelings, and even, in some cases, make use of amazing psychic and physical abilities which we are naturally endowed with. Now, I believe what Anya told me, because I can see in you what she does, and I want to offer you the opportunity to become one of us. I am not going to let you speak, not yet, because there is something you must understand before you agree."

Bartholomew straightened in his seat. "You need to know that our world is not without risk to your work life. For example, if somebody found out, people don't yet accept us and our ways. But it's also not without reward." He smiled at Jonah. "No matter how hard you try, you will never be able to tell anyone what you learn of us, after you join and up to that point. You will not speak of it, write of it… no communication will work. The knowledge lies in your head only. We have certain… persuasive measures.

This is to protect our world as well as keep it a secret. Jonah, Anya chose you for a reason. You will perhaps find out that reason later, but only when the time is right."

With a heavy sigh, Bartholomew stood and pressed a card into Jonah's hand, holding tightly onto his fist. "When you make your decision, phone this number and simply speak the word 'yes' or 'no' without a name or any form of address."

Jonah left the Manhattan at four o'clock, confused and ill at ease. When he finished with the agent at home, he could finally sit down and let his thoughts take over. Bartholomew had, at first, calmed him. By the time he had stood to leave, Jonah held him in awe.

The man had read his mind.

***

Anya slipped quietly back into the chamber where she slept after Jonah had left. It was getting late and she was tired, mentally exhausted. As she turned to lean against the door she had just shut, Alexander's voice startled her from the dark.

"What do you make of him pet?"

She turned to where he leaned casually against the frame of the large four-poster bed, shirtless and dangerous, his strong arms crossed over his muscular chest and washboard stomach. With the respect she had always held for him, and the love she always would, Anya moved slowly toward him and dropped into a kneeling pose at his bare feet.

"I think he is a lost man, Master. There is someone who has hurt him in his past that he needs to get over. He is missing something from his life, he reminds me of myself when I met you... As far as abilities go, there is something in his touch, in his hands."

When she finished her report, she bent forward and laid her face sideways at his feet.

Alexander sank to his haunches, squatting over her, and stroked her face, hair and back. "You did very well. Now come with me, let's bathe you, you smell of the club. I want you smelling only like yourself."

He lifted her to her feet and removed the ornamental wrist cuffs and collar, dropping the diaphanous fabric shift carelessly to the floor. A hot bath stood prepared, and he lifted her into the steamy water, proceeding to wash her hair and her whole body. Anya relaxed into his touch, she valued these special times, and loved it when he bathed her.

When she stood, dry, beside the bed, she watched him pick up the heavy leather collar of ownership and approach her. He buckled the soft and well-worn collar around her neck, kissed her forehead, and lifted the blankets to let her crawl into the massive bed, under soft sheets. He stripped naked and joined her, pulling her into the cradle of his arms tightly.

Just before they fell asleep he whispered, "Tonight you are tired, little one, and it is late, I can see it. But tomorrow you are mine, my plaything."

***

Anya knew she was spiralling steadily down, heading for a dark pit, when Alexander found her one night. Her friends had left, and she was sitting on the curb, barely in a fit state to know her own name, her knees together and her fingers tracing the ladders in her stocking as she stared at a cockroach running past her stiletto. A hand came to rest on her shoulder, and it was then that she noticed the thumping music had all but stopped.

"Hey, are you okay?" a deep voice asked from behind her.

Damn, some hot one, this is.

She heard footsteps, and then he knelt down in front of her as she swayed, her head spinning.

"Honestly, I don't know," she mumbled, closing her eyes. She turned away from him, nervous of throwing up on Mr. Hottie-Mc-Hotness.

He was a persistent one. "What did you take?" His voice faded into background static, and the world went grey around the edges.

"Lots." Her lips were numb. Anya felt the steel bands of his arms as he caught her, and then she felt nothing.

***

"Something for the pain," Eloise had screamed in her ear earlier, as they gyrated together on the floor. She'd pressed two bottles into Anya's hand and smiled, watching Anya empty pills into her palm.

"Hey, go easy!" Eloise had cautioned, but Anya had swatted her away, downing the pills with her vodka and cranberry. If it made the heartache go away, good. If it made her consciousness of the heartache and memory of what had happened go away, even better. Vicodin and Xanax. She'd read the bottle briefly when she went to the toilets later, as she stood staring at her gaunt reflection in the badly lit mirror. She was familiar with them both. Her own prescriptions had long run out, and the fucking psychiatrist refused to give her more.

They'd danced and drank, and she'd waved the others off, refusing to leave with them, swaying and moving with the music, finding a random guy at every turn to cling to for a while. She was a pretty girl and it was easy. They eventually left, because she wouldn't blow them or fuck them; just dance, no sex, no groping, no making out. That's how she ended up on the curb of the club alone, and high off her head, at four in the morning.

That's also how Alexander ended up finding her on his way home from a rare night out with buddies he didn't see often. He hated clubbing. He disliked the noise, the drugs that were so prevalent, not to mention the underage drinking. It was repulsive.

***

When Anya regained consciousness she was in a soft, comfortable bed. The bedroom was dimly lit, and when she opened her eyes and rubbed the sleep from them, she saw the walls were a soft grey. The bed, over-sized enough to make her feel like a midget, was plush, covered with different textures of white linen, and when she folded back the covers in a blind panic, she wore a black T-shirt and men's boxer briefs. Who in the hell's name had stripped her?

She didn't feel hung over at all, but had no recollection of anything after getting dressed to go out with her friends. This was not Eloise's place, and not Drew's. Panic set in when it hit home that she had no idea where she was. On the table beside the bed lay her purse, and when she rifled through it, it held a lot of cash, two almost-empty pill bottles, and her mobile, with a dead battery. All her stuff, nothing stolen.

Anya stood, walked quietly to the door, and with a deep breath, pushed it open to find out where the hell she was, and whose house she was in. The bedroom door opened smoothly, and had no locks on it, not even a handle. She peeped out into a long passage, painted the same pale grey, and smelled coffee. Automatically following her nose in the direction of the alluring scent, her stomach twisted up into a ball of knotted anxiety and fear of what she had done.

At the end of the passage, she came to a large, open-plan room, lined on one side by a very long counter and leather stools, which separated the space into a kitchen, a living room and dining area. Anya quietly walked over to the counter, and stood staring at a notepad which lay in the middle, a pen across the top.

There is coffee in the kitchen, please help yourself, I apologise, but I do not yet know your name. - Alexander.

"Oh God," she said, bending forward and resting her head on her arms. She had come home with a man. She hadn't yet straightened to stand when a deep voice behind her startled her so badly she jumped.

"What did God do to you so early in the morning?"

She whirled, and landed with her back to the counter. "Um, I, sorry, I guess I was hoping I had been responsible," she stuttered, staring at the shaved-headed, tattooed, T-shirt wearing god who had just entered the room. Her hormones set her body on instant alert.

He moved closer again, and Anya backed a little further away.

With a smile, he held out a hand. "I am Alexander, and I promise I won't bite. I brought you to my home when I found you outside the club, incapable of looking after yourself. I promise I didn't touch you inappropriately, merely dressed you in clean-smelling clothes so that you could sleep comfortably." He spoke kindly, as though to a feral kitten.

Anya shook his hand, noting the size of it; in comparison to hers it was massive.

"Anya, that's my name," she said softly. "Thank you Alexander, I am sorry about last night, I had a rough time and it got a bit out of hand."

He merely nodded and walked into the kitchen. "We've all been there. You haven't had coffee?" He turned to face her, and the blue of his eyes left her momentarily speechless. "Anya? Coffee?"

"I would love some, thank you." She watched intently as he reached up to a shelf, bringing down a mug and pouring strong black liquid into it.

"Do you need sugar and milk?"

Anya shook her head. He stood staring at her from across the counter as she raised the mug to her face, which was so big she practically disappeared behind it.

He spoke. "I get the feeling you are not in such a great place Anya. I usually have good instincts about people, so I am going to give you a card with my number. I want you to go away and think about what you'd like to do to get to a better place in your life, and if you want my help, with anything at all, call me. Will you do that?"

She left his house an hour later, still wearing his T-shirt over her dress from the night before. As she'd walked into her apartment, and looked at the mess, she'd broken down in tears and called him.

Through her floods of agony, she had simply said, "Please, I don't know why I am asking you, of all people, but yes, help me."

For some reason she had felt safe with him, and knew she could trust this man.

***

Anya tried not to move a muscle when she opened her eyes on Saturday morning, but Alexander was aware she was awake before she could hide herself.

"Morning kitten," he purred, gently running a hand through her hair. Anya tensed instinctively, and behind her Alexander chuckled. "Aw, so nervous, why baby?" He licked her neck.

She turned to face him. "Morning, sir. Well, I know you want to play today. I am always nervous before we do that. I don't know what to expect."

Alexander stroked her cheek. "That's good, I like you on your toes. It just occurred to me that I don't have to wait until this afternoon to play with you. I have you all day. Go and fetch your ears and tail, I want to play with my kitten, it's really the perfect morning for cuddling a little kitten in bed."

His voice had taken on a playful tone, and Anya jumped up to do as he asked. If he was in a good mood, she was going to keep him that way for as long as possible.

Her chest of toys was at the foot of the bed, and she removed the kitten tail butt-plug, a set of ears attached to a headband, and four glove-type paws. Alexander stood next to the bed, waiting for her with the bottle of lubricant in his hand, while she put on her ears along with the little hand-paws and leg-warmer paws. When she climbed on all fours onto the bed in front of him, a shiver of anticipation ran down her spine, right to her curling toes.

She went down on her elbows and wiggled her arse, presenting herself to him in the most vulnerable of ways, fully exposed. To someone new, this was one of the most humiliating positions. Anya giggled briefly as his finger applied cold lube to her, and then hushed swiftly, freezing when that finger slid oh so slowly into her body. His finger soon left, and she heard him make an appreciative sound behind her, shortly before she felt the cold steel of the plug at her tight opening.

Alexander was so experienced he could make anything pleasurable. He slowly moved it against her tense muscles. He reached his free hand up to stroke her back, distracting her attention from it entirely, and she almost purred at the contact. Her body relaxed to accept the intrusion, and Anya gasped as the widest part popped in, hollowing her back under his hand.

He chuckled again. "Hold still, pet, let me wipe the excess lube off, I don't want a mess on my sheets." He wiped her intimately with a wet-wipe, leaving her squealing at the cold and indignity.

She stayed still as he lay down on his back on top of the covers and then patted his lap, giving her the signal she'd been waiting for. Anya crawled toward him, stretching the paws gracefully ahead of her, and sprawled across his legs. She purred loudly as he ran his hands through her hair, down her spine, tugged gently at the tail, and then continued down her legs. He did that for such a long time her eyes began to drift shut. Just before she fell asleep, he pulled gently at the hair above her ears.

"Does my kitten want a saucer of milk?" he asked softly.

Anya almost spoke, stopped herself, then raised her head and let out a loud meow. Alexander shifted her gently off his lap to stand, then waited for her to follow him, all the way to the kitchen attached to these rooms, crawling on her hands and knees, making purring and meowing noises as she went. He poured milk into a saucer, placed it on the floor, and watched as she struggled to keep her hair out of the way and lap up the liquid. He bent to stroke her, and she purred again.

When she finished the milk, she sat up and groomed, cleaning her little paws as a cat would, licking, wiping her nose, which got covered in milk, then licking again. As she finished, Alexander lead her back to the bedroom and sat down at his desk, pulling a large, well-cushioned animal bed, with pink pillows and blankets, closer to his feet. He watched her curl up, petted her again and opened his laptop. Anya fell asleep content, comfortable and feeling safe.

Anya stretched and yawned a little while later, gasping when the plug shifted inside her with her movement.

Alexander smiled down at her from where he sat typing. "Hey, sleepy kitty," he said, reaching down to stroke her hair from her face.

Anya felt her bladder urging to be emptied, and grimaced. This part of the pet-play realm killed her, the particular type of loss of dignity. Alexander knew exactly how badly, so he kept her in her role until she had survived the unspeakable, almost every time they did this. It didn't happen often, so she tended to forget to relieve herself beforehand, and was usually caught unawares.

Alexander did what he did to remind her of her station as a slave, and she suffered the indignity and humiliation purely because of how happy it made him. She was always willing to do these things for him, these animal based things that left her feeling embarrassed to her core, without question. She allowed herself to be debased to please him.

She nudged his thigh, uttered a pitiful meow and stared with desperation into his smug visage as he spoke.

"Well, you know what to do, little kitten, you have been trained."

She dropped her head and crawled to the oversized pit of perfumed kitty litter in the corner of the room, just beyond his desk. She clambered carefully in and squatted there to relieve herself. At that moment, Anya had to pretend the world fell away and that nobody could see her, so she closed her eyes. Alexander was onto her mental coping mechanisms though, and came to stand beside her, carefully lifting her tail before her tinkling stream of urine fell onto the crystal litter.

Anya's back stiffened when she felt his hand. She hadn't heard him approach. Now all her concentration had to be on relaxing her bladder, and it took a while.

"Do you have performance anxiety, my pet?" He chuckled above her, and she opened her eyes, directing a malevolent glare in his direction, and hissed.

When she finally completed the task, she kicked litter from under her feet, spraying it on the carpet. While she was a kitten, Alexander looked after her, thus cleaning up the mess she made. Let him deal with that kitten mess, she thought darkly, ignoring him to go and curl up on the bed and nurse her injured dignity.

For his part, he left her to it, let her curl up on the bed and went back to his workspace, shaking his head at her stormy temper. Quite placidly, Alexander fetched a small brush and dustpan, swept the spilled litter into it and disposed of the crystals.

***

Morning turned into afternoon, and Alexander freed her from the bondage of her kitten-guise. They sat down to lunch at a local coffee shop to let her relax a bit, and he placed his hand over hers.

"You always get so angry, yet I am so proud of you for doing whatever I demand. You are a good slave to me, Anya." He brought her hand to his lips and kissed her fingers as she sat blushing, her head lowered.

"Thank you Master."

As they strolled back to the car Anya found herself watching Alexander from the corner of her eye, and saw his mood tangibly darken. They seldom spent nights at the club anymore, preferring to go home to his apartment. When the night dragged on, as last night had, the quarters he kept on the premises were a convenience she appreciated.

His apartment, a refurbished warehouse in the old harbour district, and the same place where she had woken up that Saturday morning so many years ago, was still one of the most beautiful and comfortable homes Anya knew of. She felt safe there.

Alexander's jaw was clenched tight when she glanced furtively at him, having slid comfortably into her seat and fastened the seatbelt. They drove in silence, passing several lively restaurants, the aquarium, and a few ships on the way. As the garage door opened silently, Anya wondered what had hurt his good mood.

When Alexander stopped the car in its parking spot, he turned to face her. "I want you waiting for me in front of the cross, naked. Fetch your collar, two lengths of rope in whatever colour you would like, and my two floggers."

He stepped out of the car to open the door for her, and kissed her forehead. He paused in the doorway, facing her, to take a big breath and stare deeply into her eyes.

"Anya, I love you."

Alexander left Anya standing there with those words ringing in her ears, dissolving into a puddle of nervous anticipation and aroused beyond comprehension. He said that sometimes before play that broke her, when he knew she would need to remember the fact that he loved her to hold out. Anya's hair fell across her eyes as she climbed the stairs to the basement entrance.

He would be checking on the club staff who were preparing for an event that evening, a private group, and Anya felt sure he was simply making sure they would have privacy for as long as he required it. She walked up the steps, carefully and slowly, and stopped in front of her chest of toys to pick up the floggers and her collar. She selected two lengths of deep red rope, a soft cotton variety from the basket next to her chest, and with those items in hand she left the bedroom.

***

The St. Andrews' cross stood in the central, sunken floor area, and it was made of railway sleeper wood beams, polished smooth by touch and the staff who cleaned everything daily. As Anya rested her cheek against the wood, she inhaled the comforting scent, so familiar. Goosebumps broke out along her arms when a chilly breeze caressed her naked skin, blowing from the passage to the private rooms. Her eyes fell on the floggers she had hung on hooks nearby for Alexander, and on her collar which lay on the counter. She would never put it around her neck herself, which was forbidden. Only Alexander collared her and removed it again.

When she was alone like this, waiting in anticipation for him, for play, her mind frequently dwelled on the first time she had seen his dungeon, when she was still only eighteen. Anya was lost in those memories and didn't notice him enter.

Alexander stopped when he entered the large space, standing to watch her as she stood leaning against the cross, brushing her cheek over the wood with a faint smile on her face. He knew where her mind was, and didn't mind. He fondly thought of their first months together when he was alone, too. With a deep breath he stepped into the sunken space, placing the narrow cane in his hands, just out of her sight. His boots thumped when they made contact with the floor. Anya was yanked from her reminiscing, and turned her head slightly to face him, still smiling.

She watched silently as he picked up her collar and approached her, reaching around her neck to fasten it securely with the buckle. She heard the thud of the uncoiling rope as it hit the floor, and shivered in anticipation. That sound was a mental switch for her, an instant trigger to her senses, telling her what was to come.

Alexander looped a bight of rope over her left wrist, tied a single column tie, and pulled it taut through the ring at the top of the cross's strut. He did the same with her right hand, and then both ankles, leaving her spread-eagled and vulnerable. Anya shivered in the chill breeze moving through the area. He ran his hands up her sides, from ankle to arm.

"Are you cold pet?" he asked, pressing his body to hers.

She nodded. "A little, sir."

He moved behind her and picked the lighter flogger off its hook. "Don't worry, we can fix that quite easily."

The first gentle blows licked at her shoulders, and Alexander slowly, almost lazily, worked his way down her back, her thighs, and her calves. When he started on her shoulders again, he used a little more force. Anya's breath came a little harder when he switched to the heavier flogger. He hadn't started yet, but she was trying to prepare herself mentally for the beating.

A sigh escaped her when she felt his fingers trace her spine. When his hand cupped her arse, she moaned. Alexander stood behind her, watching her torso rise with her breathing, and a thrill ran through him as she moaned at his hands on her.

This control, having this beautiful creature so willing to please him in any and every way, was what he did these things for. He certainly didn't lack control in his everyday life. With a club to run and over thirty employees, he was always in charge. Here, though, he could let go. Anya understood him and knew his desires, and she bent graciously to his every whim.

He took a few steps back, knowing the exact fall of his whip, and smiled at her gasp when the heavy suede made contact with her shoulder blades. This time he focused a lot of attention on her arse and thighs, leaving reddened welts in the wake of the thick strands. Anya did not know the cane was coming, she hadn't seen it nearby, and he liked warming her skin nicely beforehand to avoid breaking it. If he was going to make her bleed, it would be intentional and not by misjudgement or fluke.

When Alexander stopped, hanging both the whips where they belonged, Anya stood panting, and a few stray tears ran down her cheeks. He moved behind her again, and this time when he pressed himself to her, he reached around her body to cup her breasts in his hands. She writhed against him, rubbing herself on his erection, tangible through the fabric of his jeans.

He bent her head to the side with a hand in her hair, and softly kissed her neck, moving up to nibble her ear. Her neck strained as he twisted her head and kissed her. He could feel her gasp through the kisses, and when he released her, she hung limp in his arms. Alexander moved his hand down, across the soft skin of her belly, and when he ran a finger between the lips of her sex they came away slick with moisture.

His mouth at her shoulder he murmured, "Hmm, nice, my pet. I like your response to my whips."

"Please, sir, let me cum, please," she begged.

Alexander chuckled. "No, I don't think you sound quite desperate enough yet."

He stood back and picked up the cane, held it to her lips and waited. Anya whimpered, but kissed the tool, then closed her eyes. He expected the show of respect, especially for this, because he knew how she feared the cane, but making her submit to it was for his pleasure. He loved marking her with its stripes, and enjoyed the knowledge that she saw and felt them for quite a while after the actual event, a tangible reminder of his ownership.

When he stood back again, he measured where his strokes would land, running it over her already red skin gently, watching as she winced in anticipation. He drew it back and swung, leaving a vivid stripe across the top of her arse cheeks, and worked his way down while she clenched her jaw and hissed at the impact, the one just below the curve where her arse met her thighs eliciting the first loud cry from her.

Alexander changed his stance, and took the backs of her thighs one at a time, moving in rapid succession down each one, admiring the plethora of interconnected bright lines left behind. Anya was audibly crying and struggling against her restraints, but he ignored her pleas of 'stop, no more, please' because they were not her safe word. He took his time, finishing both her thighs before laying the cane aside.

Anya heard the implement touch the floor, and hid her face from him when he approached. He ran his hands over the raised welts, eliciting a fresh cry of pain from her, and then reached between her thighs again. She willingly spread herself for his hand, and moved against his fingers, soaking them with her arousal.

He left her tied, and unbuttoned his jeans, thrusting into her wet, hot and hungry sex, fast and hard. Anya cried out and arched her back at the stretch of his granite-hard cock filling her so suddenly. She sobbed when he ran his hands roughly down her welted back and over her arse, digging his short nails into her skin, but her orgasm rushed over her like a tidal wave when he reached for her clit and kneaded it roughly between his fingers. She gripped the cuffs at her wrists fiercely, hanging on, and bucked against him while her inner muscles tightened in a spasm around him. Alexander grasped her hips and grunted like a wild animal when he spilled himself into her pliant body.

Both spent, they breathed hard, and he hung onto her body, resting his face against the back of her neck,

"Still cold?" he asked mischievously.

She shook her head. "Uh uh, nope."

Anya burst into a fit of giggles. He pulled out of her body, watched her shudder, and buttoned his jeans, then started untying her gently. She stood, dazed, with his fluid running from her body. It was one of the sexiest sights Alex could ever want to see, and he gathered her into his arms, leaving the whips and tools for the staff to return to his quarters.

He carried her upstairs and lay her on the bed, immediately sitting with her and letting her curl up in his arms. Her breathing slowed and she started crying softly, wetting the fabric of his shirt with the salt of her tears.

"It's okay baby, you did so well, I am incredibly proud of you," he whispered, stroking her hair. He let her cry herself out as he continued whispering sweet things to her, and then tenderly turned her over to assess the damage to her skin. "That is going to leave some pretty markings," he said, appraisingly.

Anya tried to look, but couldn't see much. Alexander stood, fetched a tub of coco-butter body lotion, and spent about twenty minutes rubbing it into her arse and thighs. He then cuddled her on the bed until she fell asleep, covered her in soft blankets, and left her to rest.

Aftercare was something he enjoyed almost as much as actual play. For Alexander it was a time to bond with your submissive, slave or Dominant. It was a special thing, an important part of building and maintaining relationships, where so much trust was crucial. He watched her from his desk for a while, her face restful and her hair wild around her head as she lay on her side, then walked into his bathroom to shower.

Chapter 3

Jonah mentally prepared himself for a long process concerning the sale of his apartment the moment he decided he wanted to sell and move on. The economy was not great, and it was especially not a seller's market. He sighed, hating the idea that he might take a loss if he could not get his asking price. He didn't have a huge amount of savings, and was not sure about having a tremendous mortgage over his head.

As he sat at his desk now, a week after making the decision to sell, he patiently worked through an audit for a cosmetics company, searching carefully for discrepancies. His pocket vibrated as his cellular started ringing, and he frowned when he saw the estate agent's number there. He hadn't been anticipating any calls from her just yet.

"Good morning." He answered politely, keeping his voice down so as not to disturb his office companion. He clamped the phone between his shoulder and ear as he listened to her speak.

Annette, the agent, spoke fast. She had a young couple for whom she suspected his apartment would be perfect. They were both career lawyers, had no children, and liked the idea of a new, hip area. Jonah promised to leave keys with the building supervisor the next morning so she could show the apartment to them, and hung up. "

Well, what do you know," he muttered to himself. His Tuesday was set to get interesting.

Jonah glanced down at his watch and decided it was time to grab a cup of coffee, so he stood and walked to the kitchen, preoccupied with the thought of searching for a new home, and the thought that this might happen sooner than he'd anticipated. Stavros, one of his co-workers, was in the kitchen paging through the Financial Mail, and looked up at him when he pushed a mug into the Nespresso machine, slid a capsule home and pushed the button for a Grande Americano.

"What's up, Jonah? Looks like you have big things on your mind," he remarked, closing the magazine and shifting his focus to Jonah.

Jonah shrugged casually. "I put my apartment on the market a week ago, and already have a prospective buyer. I guess I just wasn't anticipating house-hunting quite so soon." He heard the uncertainty and doubt in his own voice. "I am starting to realise I am not so great with change."

Stavros laughed softly, "Don't sweat it, the first thing to think of is what you want in your next house." He crossed his arms.

"I have thought this through. I need a free standing house, so that I have privacy. I want a couple of bedrooms, space so I don't have to upgrade again soon, and a cellar so that I can store a few nice wines." He shivered at the thought of building his own version of that club's central play space.

Was he really considering this, saying yes? Jonah shook his head and refocused his attention on Stavros.

Stavros' face lit up. "You know, you should get an agent to show you the neighbourhood where I live." Jonah couldn't decide if it was a snobby comment. "It's near Sherwood Gardens and John's Hopkins University, there are a couple of really nice red-brick mini-mansion type places on sale at the moment. You might like them, depending on your budget of course."

Jonah kept it to himself, but the man's tone concerning budget had sounded decidedly snide and sarcastic. "I will do that, I might even take a drive around and see if the area suits me first."

Jonah felt new excitement about the prospect of a large house, born from his doubt and nervousness. Perhaps he could make this work, a nice new place to build new memories. He thanked Stavros and they departed to their desks to carry on with their work.

***

He walked into his apartment after work later that evening and retrieved a beer from the fridge, cracking the cap before he sat down on the couch. On his coffee table in front of him lay the card Bartholomew had handed him, the one that showed nothing but a number. He found his fingers were shaking as he picked it up, the thick board almost hot in his fingers.

Jonah knew he had to do this. He felt it in his gut and in the curious depths of his mind. He closed his eyes and pictured that blonde woman on the cross. It was so vividly engrained in his memory he could virtually hear the whip strike her flesh, and her moans of pleasure as she came later, with the tall man's hands on her.

With a flood of butterfly wings through his stomach, and a rush of blood to his head, Jonah picked up his cellular phone and dialled the number. When it was picked up without answer, he said the word he had been instructed to and nothing else.

"Yes."

He had no idea what would happen now, who would reach him, or how he would be contacted. Jonah only knew that his life was going to change, even if he didn't know how. He felt suddenly restless, put the beer down, and picked up his phone and car keys, heading out to the garage. He only drove on weekends or at night, preferring public transport to work and back. His car was a guilty pleasure. A smile involuntarily broke out on his face when he saw his baby, a Porsche 718.

Jonah had wanted a Porsche for as long as he could remember, and this one, a deep metallic blue with a cream coloured leather interior, he cherished. It had taken him two years of doing every piece of freelance work he could find over and above a full-time job, and he had saved relentlessly to afford it. His parents had not spoilt him, but taught him that things are better enjoyed when you earn them, a mentality he held onto tightly. Inside the car, as the engine purred to life, he breathed in the scent of the leather and stroked the steering wheel lovingly.

The Killers played 'Runaway' as he pulled out of his parking space and waved to the guard on duty. He loved Baltimore, and smiled as he drove toward the community of Guilford, the one Stavros had mentioned. He slowed down as he passed the rolling lawns and stared at the houses, majestic behind rough red-brick walls, with lights twinkling in most of the windows. When he rounded a bend in the road, he braked and pulled over.

Just ahead of him sat a stone Georgian, a massive house. There were no lights on, but the surrounding glow from the street lights gave it a welcoming look. The gardens were enormous, and it sat well off the street. Jonah felt an instant attraction to the place, and when his gaze swept the front wall he saw a 'FOR SALE' sign perched at the entrance gate.

"There is no way in this lifetime I could afford that house," he muttered to himself, but took the agent's details down nonetheless. It would be good to have a place to start.

It was on his way home that his phone rang, the screen on his dashboard displaying an unfamiliar number via the built-in Bluetooth system. He pushed the button on his steering wheel and answered.

"Jonah speaking."

The familiar voice on the line froze him, and he pulled over to take the call. "Good evening Jonah, it is Bartholomew Black speaking. I received news of your response, and wished to welcome you myself."

Jonah shook himself to garble a response. "Bartholomew, uh, thank you!"

Jonah didn't know how else to respond, so he waited.

Bartholomew spoke again. "I want you to be at the same club where Anya brought you, on this coming Saturday evening. If you already have other plans you will have to change them, I am afraid." He didn't sound even faintly remorseful.

Jonah chuckled. "I will be there, Mr. Black. I have no plans."

"Good. Oh, wear black if you please, or a suit if you have one."

He hung up without a greeting, leaving Jonah to sit in his car trembling in anticipation. He did not sleep much that night after tidying up the apartment for show, lying awake in his bed and staring at the ceiling until he could take it no more, and sat in his bed reading.

The next day at the office his exhaustion showed. He slumped over his paperwork, not really seeing anything, and barely spoke to anyone. He did, however, check the site belonging to the estate agent in charge of the Georgian house in Guilford. He frowned when he saw the price; compared to similar properties in the neighbourhood it was unreasonably cheap. He picked up the phone and dialled their number.

"Hi, may I speak to an agent regarding the big Georgian in Guilford?" he asked, giving her the exact address.

The receptionist transferred him straight away, and Jonah's heart sped up.

The woman who answered his call could have no idea how excited he was as she picked up. "Alice here, hello," she said in a calm and professional tone.

Jonah started rambling before he could stop himself. "Hi Alice, my name is Jonah MacPherson, and I am curious about one of the houses in Guilford, the Georgian that sits in the cul-de-sac overlooking Sherwood Gardens, I believe? Why is the asking price so low?"

"Oh, that one," she replied, hesitating a moment. "If you negotiated they would probably go even lower, but…" She trailed off, and then suddenly seemed to remember she was on the phone with a client. "Would you like a tour of the property, Mr. MacPherson?" she chirped.

Jonah agreed and was all set to see the house the following day, Wednesday. The fact that there had been a mild emphasis on the word 'you' with regards to negotiation, didn't strike him as significant until much later.

***

The following morning Jonah faked a cough and called in sick, deciding he needed some time to himself. He had never done this, purposely faking an illness to get off work, but he was extremely excited about seeing the house, and had dressed the moment he sprang out of his bed. He was ready an hour early.

Jonah arrived outside the property, parked his car and proceeded to stand at the pedestrian entrance with his hands in his pockets, waiting for the estate agent, Alice, to arrive. He stared up the rolling lawn and past the manicured gardens at the house, drinking in the beauty of the exterior, and quietly bracing himself for the interior, his imagination conjuring up the most wonderful ideas. He could not possibly guess at the true appearance though. Looking back at the gardens he quietly wondered how many staff it took to keep the place in such perfect order.

He heard a car behind him in the road, but only turned to face Alice when she greeted him.

"Hi, you must be Jonah MacPherson?" she asked tentatively.

He smiled and nodded. "Yes, hi Alice."

Alice was a minute girl and had a narrow waist with curves in all the most strategic places. Her breasts were small beneath her blouse, and her legs shapely as they extended from the hemline of her skirt at her knees. Long, blonde hair fell in a heavy cascade down her back, and she walked with a very seductive, hip-swaying gait that reminded him vaguely of something.

She unlocked the gate and gestured for him to enter. "Shall I show you your new home?"

He followed her, trying not to get too excited before being realistic. "Slow down now, let's see if it suits my needs first, the asking price might be lower than expected, but still potentially out of my reach," he said.

Alice's musical giggle led him up the paved path as she said, almost too softly for him to hear, "Oh Mr. MacPherson, I know it will suit both you and your budget…"

***

Even standing in the entrance foyer, Jonah knew he had to have it. He glanced to his left, where a large billiard table stood framed on a wood-mosaic floor, the baize on the table glowing a deep emerald green under the soft yellow lighting when Alice started flicking switches to illuminate the house. The colour immediately made him think of Anya's eyes, and he pictured her spread naked on the table with ease.

He shook his head as his stomach clenched itself into a tight ball. He followed Alice into a large kitchen, where she stopped and placed her hands on her narrow hips.

"Let's start with the kitchen shall we? It comes with all the appliances built in. As you can see they are concealed within cupboards. There is an oven, dishwasher, clothes washer and dryer, refrigerator and wine cooler." She used a perfectly manicured finger to point them out as she spoke. "There is a separate scullery through there." She pointed out a door in the farthest corner.

"I like the size, and having appliances already here is convenient. Less shopping, I hate that." He walked around and checked the condition of all the counters: warm, dark brown granite and mahogany wood finishes.

It was truly a gorgeous kitchen, a chef's dream. Alice watched him attentively, looking to see his reaction as he laid eyes on each feature of the house. She swayed her hips, a feature to her walk enhanced by Louboutin heels, as she led him into the games room where the billiard table stood, aware of the effect this room had on men. Alice stopped next to the table, ran a hand along the baize and looked up at Jonah.

"This is obviously the games room, a very grown-up one at that. The table comes with the house as it was custom built on the premises and is too large to move. There is a bar, too, and if you look through there" —she gestured to a doorway and a set of steps— "you have a private study and library, with a reading nook and floor to ceiling shelves. It's double volume as it extends to the roof, and there are stairs."

This room was something Jonah was curious about, and he strolled in that direction, touching the wood panelling along the wall as he went. In the doorway to the library he stopped, gaping at the giant desk, leather armchair, Persian carpet and artfully placed vase of yellow roses on the small table nearby.

He turned to Alice, "Do any of the furnishings in this room come with the house?"

She nodded. "Indeed, the desk is a feature of the room, and was, just like the billiard table, built on the premises."

Jonah took out his phone. "That is nice." He rubbed his chin, deep in thought. "Listen, do you mind if I take a photo of the décor, because if I end up purchasing the house I would like to mimic this." He circled his finger to take in the room. "It works."

Alice moved closer. "Of course you may."

He snapped a picture and then followed Alice from the room. She led him into a passageway off the foyer, and toward a set of closed, heavy wooden doors. When she pushed them open and walked into the living room, Jonah's heart thundered in his chest.

"This is the most beautiful room I have ever set foot in," he said, his breath catching in his throat.

The furnishings were all deep, blue velvet, the coffee table a piece of driftwood with a glass top. Alice moved to a fireplace at one end of the room, the focus for the chairs and couches, and with the flick of a switch she set a warm fire glowing. The floors gleamed, natural wood also, polished glassy smooth. Jonah raised his head to look at the chandelier, delicate crystal teardrops laced together and hanging low over the coffee table.

Jonah had no response that could do justice to this room, it simply took his breath away. He silently followed Alice out and up an ornate flight of stairs, straight into the bedroom, the room which immediately sealed the deal for him.

A massive four poster bed sat in the centre of the floor, with a high side tables at its head. The framework looked heavy, and he approached it to run his fingers over the grain of the wood.

"Alice, does this bed come with the house?" he asked, his voice soft.

She came to stand opposite him, with a hand on the waist high surface, and looked down at the luxurious coverings. "It does, once again. It's a custom built piece and too much trouble to move. Actually, all the beds in the house are similar and will be left. If you want, I can let the owners know they can leave any furnishings they aren't taking? If you like the stuff."

"I love everything." He turned, the atmosphere was charged with sexual tension as Alice kept her focus on him. He walked to a large bay window directly opposite, overlooking the back gardens and Sherwood Gardens beyond. "Why is the asking price on the house so low? And at that, with all these beautiful furnishings included…" Jonah trailed off as he stood looking out.

Alice again came closer. "The owners are in the process of a divorce, sadly, and want to wrap things up, as the wife is emigrating and the value needs to be split. It's all rather unfortunate. They were a little strange when I met them."

She sounded puzzled, and he turned to face her. "How so?"

Alice frowned. "Well, the wife was so quiet, so demure. She never looked directly at me, she only spoke when he addressed her, and he seemed to, I don't know, control her…"

Jonah felt tingles run down his spine. From his research, it sounded like a dominance and submission dynamic; he found it funny that Alice would find it abnormal. He had certain suspicions about this girl.

"Oh, that is strange." he mumbled. "I want this house, Alice, and I would like to make an offer on it right now."

She nodded. "Of course. The asking price is two point nine million dollars, but honestly, I reckon they will accept anything over two, just to be done with it. I suggest you start at two and see what they say. We haven't had any interest in the property, and it's been on the market for a month, but they want a speedy sale and are not exactly poorly off."

"Perfect. I will do an offer of two million exactly, let me know what the response is."

They left the room, and Alice stopped him. "But you haven't seen the basement, or the rest of the house?" She sounded disappointed.

Jonah nodded. "I know, but I want it regardless. I will walk through it now and look at everything else. Contact the sellers and tell them right away, if you don't mind."

Jonah wandered through the house on his own, loving every single detail. He came to a door with a brass plaque on it, reading 'basement' and pushed it open to enter the cool darkness beyond.

"Is there a light switch?" he asked, feeling his way along the wall, blinking when Alice pulled a cord behind him to illuminate the stairwell.

"I got their voicemail, but I'll try again later and be in touch regarding the cost." Alice stood close to him, her breath sweet and warm, her eyes shining. "Come."

She beckoned, excitement in her voice as she passed him to sashay down the stairs. He stumbled down behind Alice, still partially blinded, and when his eyes adjusted he had to gaze around him for quite a few moments before he fully realized what he was looking at. It was a perfectly laid out dungeon.

***

"They left it kitted out like this. I mean, there are no toys or anything, that would be gross. But the furniture is here,"

Alice said, as she walked over to the leather-upholstered cross mounted on the farthest wall.

Jonah stood frozen, his gaze running from the cross, to a bench, to chains dangling from the ceiling. His heart pounded in his throat as he saw a large, leather armchair in one corner, on a Persian rug, and a small table and bookshelf at its side.

"Fuck," he muttered, wiping the beads of perspiration from his brow, where they had suddenly formed. "They have a fully kitted out fucking dungeon." He was speaking more to himself, but looked across at Alice. "Excuse my language, but you knew this and didn't tell me?"

Alice turned her back toward the cross, leaning against it to reach up and grip the restraints casually. "I wanted to see your face when you first saw this. It catches most people a little off-guard," She was flirting with him, outrageously so.

"Did you now?"

A sense of cockiness rolled over him and he moved closer, near enough to touch her, stroked the leather cross behind her and saw the lust in her big, blue eyes. This was the first time he had really noticed how pretty the girl was. She looked very young at that moment.

She sidled up to him and snaked her arms around his neck. "I did, yes," she said.

Before Jonah could gauge her next move, soft, warm lips were on his. He closed his eyes and savoured the feel of her silken mouth, her breasts pressing against his chest and her fingers in the hair at the back of his neck. He felt her hard nipples through the thin fabric of her blouse.

Reality interrupted, swiftly shaking him from his enjoyment, and Jonah gently pushed Alice away.

"I can't do this, I am sorry Alice, my life is complicated right now, and if I end up hurting you…" He ran a hand through his hair and turned away.

Her giggles puzzled him. "Don't worry, it's only a kiss. I get excited when I look at this room and the stuff in it, it makes me curious about what kinds of things people might get up to in here." She seemed completely nonplussed, and led him from the basement. Jonah had never come across a woman who so casually dismissed a rebuttal.

"Now, I know there are parts of the house you haven't seen, would you like to? Or shall we see what comes from the offer? I am happy to arrange another tour, I don't mind."

She stopped at the top of the stairs and straightened her skirt, then glanced at him, still smiling.

Jonah felt thoroughly ruffled and couldn't think straight. "Um, yes, I mean, let's just see what happens, I have a few things I need to get done today."

He followed her through the house to the foyer. She bid him farewell while she turned back to go in and switch off the lights, along with the fire she had demonstrated for him, still burning in the living room.

"I will be in touch Jonah," she had said, waving a small hand.

***

Jonah's head spun when he sat down in his car. Between the overwhelming desire he had to own this house, and the bewildering, unexpected physical experience with Alice, he didn't know what to make of it all. He drove home in a slight daze, and sat in the parking garage with his head resting on his steering wheel for a solid few minutes. His nose was still filled with the smell of Alice's perfume, his mind reeled with images of Anya and the club, and thoughts of the upcoming initiation night. He still had no idea what any of it entailed, and the not knowing part of things always left him unsettled.

When he got to his apartment the light on his answering machine blinked red, letting him know that there was a massage. He pushed the replay button and stood listening, getting the next shock of the day.

"Good afternoon, Mr. MacPherson. I have news regarding your apartment, if you would please return my call soon." It was the voice of his own estate agent, and from her tone, she was excited about something.

He picked up the phone and dialled Annette.

She answered almost instantly. "Mr. MacPherson! I have such good news, you know the young couple I showed your apartment to? Well, they want to offer you one point six million."

Jonah choked on his own spit. "I'm sorry, how much?" he gasped.

Annette chuckled. "I realise it is a high offer, but they really want to make sure the apartment goes to nobody else. Are you happy with that?"

Jonah struggled to find his voice, but eventually laughed out loud. "Hell yes, I'll take that offer, it's perfect. Thank you, this is amazing."

She promised to email him the relevant paperwork and then hung up. He thought his surprises for the day were over until his cellular rang in his pocket, and he answered it to hear Alice's voice.

"Hi handsome," she purred.

So the flirting was still on.

Jonah held his phone away to stare at it for a moment, and then replied, "Hi Alice, what's up?"

She giggled, which seemed to be her go-to response for everything. How could such cheerfulness not promote sales, Jonah thought. "I called to congratulate you. Your offer was accepted and you are now the owner of a beautiful, big house, with a kinky dungeon."

He sat down, hard, in the nearest chair. "Oh my God."

It was more of a murmur than an answer, but she still responded. "Go and celebrate, Mr. Macpherson. Have a bottle of champagne, tell everyone the good news and start planning your décor! You can move in within the next two weeks." She sounded genuinely happy for him, and hung up with a happy greeting.

It was much later in the day, early evening in fact, after he had told his parents about the house and had a shower, when he sat back on his couch with a beer, processing all the sudden changes. He dreaded the paperwork to come, but hoped it would be swiftly wrapped up, having already dealt with his own apartment's side of things.

When Jonah's phone rang again, for what felt like the hundredth time, he was sorely tempted to ignore it. He looked at the screen, which showed a blocked number, and answered anyway, with a heavy sigh. He wasn't quite sure why. "MacPherson, hello."

"Jonah, how delighted I am that you answered. Most people show complete disdain for blocked numbers, how are you lad?" It was Bartholomew Black, and Jonah smiled to himself at the familiarity the man showed, using the term 'lad' so easily.

"Good evening, Bartholomew, I am well thank you. It's been a surprising, well, a great day." He couldn't help but chuckle, he truly was happy, but why was this man calling him? "Is there anything you need?"

Bartholomew didn't hesitate on the other end of the line. "Why, no. Other than still being overjoyed that you will be with us on Saturday, I merely wished to congratulate you on the purchase of your new home, and wish you joy in the years to come."

Jonah's breath caught He started to speak and then calmed his tone; he was still deeply wary of these people. "How did you know?"

He walked into his kitchen, leaned against the counter and rubbed his forehead as he remembered the feeling that Bartholomew had read his mind at their last encounter.

There came a mild laugh from Bartholomew. "Do you not think the house may have been owned by someone in our... How do I put this, organisation? Or that your pretty little estate agent may be affiliated with us? For that matter, perhaps your own apartment's buyers may have had incentive to purchase your place…" He trailed off, leaving Jonah confused. He hadn't even thought of these things.

Jonah had no response, so Bartholomew continued. "I shall see you on Saturday, Jonah, don't be late." With that he hung up.

Jonah stared at his phone, dropped it carelessly on the counter and walked into his bedroom. "I give up," he muttered. He brushed his teeth and slid into his bed. He had had more than enough excitement for one day.

Chapter 4

Saturday afternoon found Jonah standing in front of his closet, panicking about what to wear. "Black," he mumbled. "Something black."

He ended up in chinos and a collared shirt with the sleeves rolled up. It was far from formal, but he had no tux lying around. He reached for a jacket and carefully brushed the lint from it, threw it over his arm and headed for the door. Jonah slid into his car and switched on the radio, and then was on his way to the club.

He was tense and on edge, not knowing what to expect.

***

At the club, all was dark. It was exactly as Jonah remembered: a creepy and run down old mansion. He raised his hand to knock on the door, but it opened as he did so. The same man who had last greeted him bowed and stepped aside to let Jonah enter.

"Good evening Mr. MacPherson, if you have a seat I will call an escort for you, to lead you to where the others are waiting."

Jonah's brow furrowed. "The others?"

The older man nodded. "The initiates, sir."

He spoke as though Jonah should know exactly what he meant and turned away, walking toward the heavy doors which led into the rest of the maze-like building. The couch was the same, the carpet was the same. Nothing here had changed. Jonah sat down, marvelling as before at the deep colour and soft textures, and as he stared at the plush fabric below his fingers, the door opened again. It took a moment for Jonah to realise the girl who followed the, well, 'butler' for all purpose and intent, was Alice.

The flirtatious young estate agent smiled demurely at him now, and bowed to him. "Good evening, Jonah."

"Alice?" he stammered, bending to look at her face.

She raised herself up to stand tall, still only reaching just below his shoulder. "Yes."

He shook his head. "Leave it to Bartholomew to tell the truth…" He trailed off as Alice turned to start towards the door.

When they entered the main floor, Jonah stood gaping at the crowds. The room was filled with formally clad men and women, and he almost lost track of Alice.

The slaves, such as Alice clearly was, wore the garb he had seen Anya in that very first night. Alice was cuffed at wrists and ankles, and a matching ornate gold collar sat at her throat, joined by a diaphanous pale pink, chiffon piece of fabric. Jonah suddenly remembered something he had noticed about her walk when she'd shown him the house. She moved the same way all the other slaves did, extremely gracefully, with a specific gait. He would have to learn about that.

She led him through the crowd and stopped in front of another heavy wooden door, turning to face him. "This is where I leave you for now, Jonah. You are expected downstairs, the Masters will be waiting." Alice kissed his cheek tenderly and pushed the door open in front of him. "I hope to see you after…"

She watched him descend the stairs, and then the door swung shut. Jonah looked around at the walls of rough stone and the lit torches in iron sconces, at intervals. It felt medieval.

The sound of Gregorian-type chanting, along with muted voices, floated toward him, and as he stepped onto the floor, several faces turned to him. A tall man with hair as black as the cloak he wore approached Jonah, and extended a hand.

"Good evening, my name is Master Gregor, and who might you be?" His tone was polite, but reserved.

Jonah shook the proffered hand. "Good evening, I am Jonah MacPherson."

"Jonah, if you'd step this way with me for a moment. Before I introduce you to the other initiates, I will give you the basics of what will happen this evening."

He placed a hand on Jonah's elbow to guide him to a quiet corner. They stopped in a quiet corner, and after a brief glance at the people in the room, mostly men, Jonah turned to Gregor, who was patiently waiting for his attention.

"Sorry, this is a little overwhelming," Jonah blurted.

Gregor seemed kind, and beckoned to a slave somewhere behind Jonah.

"This is the evening of your initiation, Jonah. This cloak will be yours from now on." A slave bowed to Jonah and handed him a thick, black cloak, similar to the one Gregor wore. "You will wear it when you bow to accept your mentor, and you will wear it every time you come here; it shows that you are one of us."

Jonah nodded, flung the thick cloak around his shoulders, surprised by the softness and weight of it, and fastened the clasp at his throat. Gregor gestured for him to follow, and led him to the group of men nearby, all looking very uncertain and hesitant.

"Jonah Macpherson," Gregor said, waiting for the other men to face him. "These are the other initiates of the Realm tonight: Anderson, Damian, Bryce, Michael and Bailey."

They all nervously shook hands and faced Gregor again without a word.

Gregor smiled, looking from one to the next before speaking. "You will all form a circle, standing on the markings." He gestured to figures carved in the stone floor. "Follow your instincts to which carving you are most drawn to. They hold significance you are not yet aware of and speak to individual men and women differently. A Master has been chosen for each of you, according to what we know of you, and he will present the chalice to you, to drink your acceptance." Gregor paused, a dramatic silence ensuing, and then looked grave. "If you refuse, you will leave and never return to this place."

The music changed, the mood along with it. Celtic drums made Jonah's sternum vibrate in his chest, and he jumped at the sudden turn from gentle chanting. Jonah watched Gregor lift his gaze to another man at the other end of the room. When he nodded, Gregor spoke only two words. "It's time."

Jonah looked at all the carvings and stepped toward one in particular he could not look away from: a side on, two-faced head wearing the Greek Laurel around both brows. The faces were gentle, and placed soft, gentle thoughts in Jonah's mind, thoughts of his changing life in a positive aspect. His nervousness and the fear he had felt about all the new things in his life fell away as he stepped onto it. He closed his eyes, waiting.

Jonah stood as still as he could in the circle, trying to keep his breathing calm. There were six of them, the new ones, in the basement, and Jonah had not met any of them until moments ago. He could hear his own heart beating in his ears over the rhythmic pounding and chanting of the Celtic music the Masters had chosen for the ritual. It filled his head even though the volume had gradually been lowered. One of the Masters passed between the new initiates, his heavy cloak brushing the floor, and everyone was silenced.

The man who walked amongst them Jonah recognised as Gregor. He stopped in the middle of the circle and started addressing them all, facing each one in turn.

"Welcome, tonight's initiates, to The Forgotten Realm. We accept you into our fold with open arms. Long may you be with us, and may you cherish the unique gifts of your decided Master."

He reached toward each man, one at a time placing a hand on their shoulder. "Jonah, Anderson, Damian, Bryce, Michael and Bailey." He spoke their names as he touched them.

As expected and instructed, a different Master approached each man, holding a chalice of wine, and in the ritual gesture, raised it to the initiate, the heavy folds of his cloak rubbing velvet against velvet as he moved.

"Drink, and take me as your teacher," they all said simultaneously. Jonah knew this was the moment in which he had to decide, even though he had never met the man in front of him. It was now or never. Either he stayed and entered the dark world of his deepest fantasies and desires, or he left and returned to his vanilla life, forsaking all the delicious possibilities The Forgotten Realm held, barred forever from its premises.

Jonah looked up into the eyes of the man he would obey and learn from. Without a smile he accepted the chalice, their fingers brushing in passing. Jonah lifted it to his lips, drinking deeply of the ruby red wine, tasting the heady Bordeaux, along with something else he could not identify, a sweet yet metallic taste.

The smile on his chosen Master's face sent shivers down Jonah's spine, and the expression in his ice-blue eyes made Jonah nervous.

"Hello Jonah," he said, his voice as cold as the glacial blue of his eyes. He held Jonah's stare, and then, unexpectedly, his smile widened and his entire demeanour changed.

It took a few moments before the power started to flow through Jonah. His eyes closed as he felt warmth rush through his veins, starting at the soles of his feet and ending at his fingertips, raising the hair at the back of his neck. He dropped his head back and stood there with his arms hanging at his sides, the chalice back in Alexander's hands.

Alexander handed the chalice to a passing slave and put his hands on Jonah's shoulders. Only then did he speak. "How do you feel?" he asked as he gazed intently into Jonah's eyes once he raised his head and re-opened them.

Jonah smiled, a little dazed, and answered with the most appropriate and honest word he could think of.

"Alive."

It was only after this, when his senses returned to him, that Jonah noticed one of the initiates being escorted from the basement, his cloak gone.

"He didn't accept his chalice. It's Bailey. It's a shame, but it always happens," Alexander said. He continued after a deep breath. "We knew by his choice of Ares's carving. They never stand the test of time." He said no more, even when he saw the puzzled expression on Jonah's face.

All the drama of the moment passed as the Masters led their new apprentices off to private areas to get to know each other. Jonah followed Alexander up the stairs and into the strange music of the main club floor. It was not too loud, and it was hypnotic, the words extremely graphic and descriptive. He didn't know where he was being led, but he did notice how the crowds parted. Every person in the vicinity bowed to Alexander.

Alexander took Jonah to a private balcony and snapped his fingers as he sat down in an armchair, gesturing for Jonah to do the same. A slave unknown to Jonah appeared, as if by magic, prostrating herself at the other man's feet, hands outstretched and forehead on the floor. Her high ponytail, of deep red hair, fell over her shoulder as she laid her head to the carpet.

Alexander bent to lift her face and spoke gently. "Persephone, please bring my companion and I one of the best single-malt scotches we have. No ice, only bottles of chilled spring water."

There was no please or thank you, simply a polite order.

Alexander watched Persephone crawl away, standing only once she was three feet away. "You stood on the carving of the Roman God Janus. Do you know the symbolism behind that?" Alexander asked, his hands crossed over a flat stomach. The cloak he wore pooled at his feet, as did Jonah's. It was a heavy and comforting sensation, he didn't know why, and Alexander seemed to wear it as naturally as skin.

Jonah shook his head. "I don't really know anything about mythology, Roman or Greek."

"I didn't expect you to be, but here's the basic idea. Janus symbolises beginnings and endings, transitions.

Your life is changing very fast, and you felt overwhelmed by it all, didn't you?"

Shivers ran down Jonah's arms. "I feel overwhelmed, but standing on that carving, all the unpleasant emotions drained from me. How is all of this happening? I am so confused by this place, by the first girl I met here, by the stuff that seems supernatural and unreal, by Bartholomew Black. I mean, what is he?"

Jonah sat forward with his head in his hands and breathed heavily. "I feel as though I don't know who I am, but that being here will help me find out."

When he felt Alexander's hand on his back, he stiffened. Jonah thought of himself as straight, which made physical touch involving men very awkward.

Alexander's voice was calming when he spoke. "It is normal to be confused and scared during a multitude of change and chaos, Jonah, which is why you have me to guide you." He removed his hand and sat back. Their drinks were placed on the table between them. Alexander had surely sensed Jonah's mild revulsion at the contact.

When Jonah took a sip of the silky smooth scotch, he noticed for the first time how handsome Alexander was, and how muscular. The strength of his arms was apparent when his cloak slid up to his elbows, revealing tattoos on both forearms.

"What is on your mind, Jonah MacPherson?" Alexander asked, and with a deep breath Jonah tried to explain.

"I do not know what I am up against here, Alexander, and at this moment I am even more confused, because I have always considered myself straight. I am drawn to you in a way I can't explain. It scares me." Jonah felt himself blush as he said this.

With a relaxed chuckle Alexander sat forward, resting his elbows on his knees. "I understand, trust me. I have been in your position. Sexuality is something we define as we grow in our experiences, it fluctuates and changes, and you shouldn't let what parents or society condition us to accept as the norm hold you back. I want to know what you want to experience, Jonah. How do you want me to teach you?"

Jonah stared long and hard at Alexander before he answered. "I want to know what the girl I saw the first night I came here experienced. I saw her being flogged. I Googled what it was, and she looked euphoric, during and after, when the man she was with touched her. I want to be a good Dominant, but I am the type who learns best from experience. I want to know what a submissive is feeling when I do things to them. I don't merely want to know the technicalities, or see written theory in a book." He sipped his drink. "Does that make any sense?"

Alexander nodded and placed his drink on the table. "Do you want to feel what she felt tonight?"

The expression on his face sent chills down Jonah's spine, and his voice almost failed him. "Yes please."

Alexander stood, and Jonah followed him from the seated area and up a flight of stairs.

By the time they reached Alexander's private quarters, Jonah's heart was again pounding in his ears; he was both scared and excited. He didn't know which emotion held the highest value.

Alexander walked up to a cross. "Take off your cloak and shirt, Jonah, and then come over here."

He spoke while Jonah stripped with shaking hands. "If anything becomes too much, and you need me to stop, the word 'red' is accepted as a safe word throughout this club, and with me in general play, no matter who I am with. You understand the concept of a safe word?" Jonah nodded and he continued. "I am going to flog you, and it will hurt, but not much. Jonah, I will touch you. What are your limits? What do you find unacceptable?"

Jonah answered without hesitation. "Sex. I am not gay."

Alexander chuckled. "Yes, I caught that. Anything else that applies?"

Jonah shook his head and slowly, warily, he approached the cross, watching Alexander pick up four, heavy leather cuffs.

As he approached, Alexander stopped him. "Breathe slowly, in through your nose and out through your mouth. Stay in the moment and allow yourself to relax into the experience. You have one word that will stop everything. Don't forget that."

Chapter 5

Jonah breathed slowly, in through his nose and out through his mouth, as Alexander had instructed him. He closed his eyes and leaned his forehead against the cool concrete of the wall, between the upper struts of the cross, as leather cuffs were tightened around his wrists. He tried very hard not to recoil when Alexander raised the hems of his chinos to attach cuffs to each of his ankles. The thought that he was being touched by another man was always going to be a big mental obstacle for Jonah.

He started when he felt Alexander's hand on the back of his neck, and his voice right in his ear. "I am going to blindfold you now, Jonah. I want you to forget your surroundings. Remember the safe word we discussed?" He spoke calmly as he fastened thick black fabric over Jonah's eyes. The scent of Alexander's skin and cologne brought feelings to light in Jonah that he had never anticipated.

"Yes, I do." His voice sounded unexpectedly hoarse to his own ears. He had not been instructed to call Alexander sir, because strictly, this wasn't submission, it was an experience. Jonah was allowing himself to learn what it would be like to feel the things a submissive would experience at his hands, one day.

The restraint panicked Jonah, and Alexander saw him struggle with the cuffs. His breathing seemed a bit more erratic than calm. Alexander knew Jonah didn't wish to appear scared or weak, but an experience like this would leave anyone nervous at first.

Alexander placed a hand on the centre of Jonah's back. "Jonah, slow your breathing. I am right here, I will not leave you alone. Okay?" He ran his hand slowly down Jonah's back when he saw the affirmative nod, smiling at the gooseflesh left in the wake of his touch.

When the heavy suede strands of the flogger dropped to the floor, Alexander saw Jonah jump at the sound. Nothing gave him more of a thrill than introducing someone to the beauty of flogging, and the euphoria of the rush that inevitably came after. He marked his distance by swinging the whip gently a few times, to gauge how close he needed to be, and then he let the first heavy thud fall on the pale skin of Jonah's shoulders.

The only sound that came from Jonah was a slightly muted grunt, with every fall of the suede strands. Alexander slowly worked his way up and down the length of Jonah's back, leaving welts on the muscles, from his shoulder-blades to above the waistband of his pants. Alexander continued until he saw Jonah's head sag forward, and the grunts stopped, replaced by heavy and methodical breathing.

When he approached Jonah, he saw the young man biting his lip.

"Have you had enough, Jonah?" Alexander asked, but no answer came. Alexander grasped Jonah's hair and pulled his head up. He removed the blindfold and looked into Jonah's eyes as he twisted his head sideways. "Answer me, have you had enough?" Alexander repeated the question, more gently this time.

Jonah blinked. "I want to say yes, please stop, but I also don't, I'm not sure," he mumbled.

Alexander smiled. The man's eyes were slightly glazed over, and he was probably experiencing one hell of an endorphin rush.

"Well that was fast," Alexander said, unbuckling Jonah's ankles first, then his wrists. He led him to a couch and handed him a glass of water. "Drink," he said, sitting down next to Jonah. "Jonah, aftercare is important, and I know you might feel a bit odd…" Alexander hadn't even finished when Jonah lay down and put his head on his lap.

"I hope you don't mind, this just seems right," Jonah said. As Alex stroked his hair, Jonah reached up and held his hand. "Thank you Alexander. I know to you that must have seemed like nothing, but it was, just… wow."

"It was not nothing. For your first time, you handled yourself well. I am not exactly gentle." Alexander released Jonah's hand and ran his fingers along a few of the welts on his back. "Sit up, let me have a better look at my handiwork."

Jonah sat up and turned his back on Alexander, shivering when Alexander ran both his hands firmly down his back, squeezing the muscle, where there would be some nice bruising, and smiling when Jonah flinched. He ran his hands up to Jonah's neck and held them around it, seeing him relax into the grip.

"Jonah, I think you're a switch."

Jonah turned around. "I cannot explain what I am feeling right now, but there is something I really want to do. I hope I don't offend you."

With that, he dropped to the ground in front of Alexander, placed his hands on Alexander's thighs, and leaned in close.

Their lips made contact for the first time. Alexander still held his hands loosely around Jonah's neck.

Alexander tightened his grasp before saying, "No offense taken, but don't do anything you will regret in the morning, Jonah." Alexander forced Jonah's mouth open, to explore it with his tongue, tasting the scotch they had had before coming into the dungeon.

Jonah didn't know where to place his hands, and grasped the muscular sides of Alexander's body, clinging to him through his shirt, as though for dear life. He lost his senses. Alexander's mouth was velvet on his, his tongue forceful yet careful. Jonah felt one hand move from around his throat and twist in his hair, and uttered a strangled cry as his head was yanked back hard.

"Is that what you needed?" Alexander growled in his ear. "Straight boy? Are you sure about being straight?"

Jonah closed his eyes. "I am not sure about anything anymore," he said, and then, when the reality of the situation really hit home, he said the one word that he knew would end everything. "Red."

Alexander released him and sat him back down on the couch, where he leaned forward, his head on his knees.

"It's okay, don't worry about a thing. You are going to feel overwhelmed in the beginning. I know, because I've been there."

***

"Let's go back to the main floor, Jonah. It is late, and I need to check what is happening with the rest of the initiates. I don't think anyone else leapt into learning as fast as you and I." Alexander had not removed any clothing for the flogging, but stood back to watch Jonah dress.

Alexander was happy with Anya's insight about choosing the man; he could see the confusion wreaking havoc on the younger initiate, but sensed he would be fine. Alexander walked straight to a slave wearing pale ice-white, with her collar and cuffs, and spoke to her quietly while Jonah looked on. Everything was well, and all his staff were present, so he could leave for the night. He stroked her back, kissed her cheek and moved back to Jonah.

"Jonah, it is quite late. I am retiring for the night, I wish to be home as I have administration to do. Are you okay?"

Jonah nodded. "I feel fine, and I think going home is a good idea for me, too. I have so much to think about."

Jonah felt deflated, confused, and wanted to escape the noise. Alexander patted his back and Jonah flinched. His skin felt abused. He looked around, not seeing Anya anywhere, and looked up at Alexander.

"Where is the girl who brought me here the first time? Anya?" he asked.

Alexander leaned closer to answer. "She is at home, it has been a very busy week for her at work, and I decided to be nice." When Jonah looked at him, puzzled, he continued. "She is my slave, Jonah, she has been for several years. You will meet her again soon, as she will be one of the women you use to practice the skills I teach you."

The thought was tough for Jonah to grasp. "You would share your woman with another man?"

Alexander nodded. "Yes, we live an open, polyamorous lifestyle, and frequently have other people in our lives. The only thing that never changes is her status as my slave. She will serve no other in the same way."

The fact that he sounded as logical as he did (Jonah momentarily pictured Spock, with his deadpan face and pointy ears) served to make Jonah more uncomfortable with the idea.

It was obvious to Alexander, too. He walked toward the door, leading Jonah. "I will explain more at a later stage. For now, get home safely and rest assured I will be in touch. Here is my mobile number."

He handed Jonah a card. When Jonah looked up, he thought for a moment he saw his gym partner walking by, leading the red-haired girl. It had looked so much like Blaine under the hood of the cloak, but he instantly dismissed the thought. It couldn't have been…

His thoughts were interrupted by Alexander's voice. "I have my bike parked in our private garage, where I presume your car is too. Drive safely. Take care, now."

Jonah took a deep breath. "Thank you Alexander, for tonight."

"Call me Alex, okay? Less of a mouthful." He left Jonah in the entrance foyer, and vanished back into the club.

The doorman held the heavy outer door for Jonah, and bowed as he bid him goodnight. Jonah walked to his car, sat heavily in the driver's seat and let his head fall back against the headrest.

***

Anya sat at the oak-wood desk in her home office, her feet bare on the plush, cream coloured carpet. It was late, but she had case studies to read through before she saw her patients the next day. She lived with Alexander in his gigantic, warehouse-type home, and for her twentieth birthday he had led her blindfolded to a door with a pink bow on it, removed the blindfold, and watched her face break into a large smile as she opened it. The room was a haven of cream and white, with accents of her favourite colour, apple green.

Alexander had laid out a large room to be her private sanctuary for study, and escape from the world, when she needed it. She rubbed her eyes now, and gazed lovingly around the room. Her desk sat facing the door. It was a large piece of furniture, and a window behind her provided daytime light. Heavy cream velvet drapes covered the glass to cut out glare when she worked on her PC. Her chair was a European white leather creation, of the most insane comfort.

One entire wall stood lined with bookshelves, and a reclining, moulded day bed decorated the corner opposite from where she sat. A chenille throw was casually draped over the edge of the leather upholstery. Anya laughed as she thought how cliché the piece of furniture was. It was the type of item that decorated every movie-psychiatrist's office…

She looked down at the pile of papers before her and sighed; she was deeply exhausted after one of the most strenuous weeks in a long time, and could not focus properly any more. Her psychology practice was a haven for victims of various kinds of abuse, and Anya's reputation had drawn teenage girls, with struggles of all kinds, to her door. Being able to help these young women made Anya happy, and every time she walked through the doors of her practice she marvelled at how far Alexander had helped her come, from a wrecked eighteen year old girl on the sidewalk so many years ago. He had encouraged her to study, paying for everything. He had taught her to love herself.

Now, having grown so much, she held a degree and owned her own business. Tonight was a welcome reprieve, and she was grateful not to have had to witness the initiation. The gawking young men generally had no concept of how to behave. Alexander understood that her work was emotionally demanding, and gave her the rest she needed. They had a relationship filled with give and take, and he was a Master who loved her just as deeply as she loved him.

She smiled now as she thought of how he had given her a bedroom of her own, after she had called him asking for his help, how he had refused to be sexually intimate with her until she was twenty-three. He had sent her to therapy and helped her deal with her past issues, and when the time came he no longer refused her. There was no fear. Only love.

Anya had gone five years without sex, and was no virgin, so she survived the frustration of celibacy with masturbation. She blushed and wished the earth would swallow her the day she found a beautifully wrapped Lelo vibrator on her bed, after school. The ensuing talk had been eye opening to her, and strengthened her love for Alexander even more.

Anya's legs ached from sitting for so long; she stretched out, stood, and walked to the kitchen. She put out a mug and placed a chamomile teabag in it.

The front door opened and Alexander came in. He looked tired, even she could see that. She automatically retrieved a second mug, and when she turned around he stood in the doorway.

"Hello, oh handsome Master," she greeted him, stepping into his arms and kissing him.

"Good evening, little one." He hugged her tightly. "I missed you tonight, did you get to finish the work you needed to do?" He kissed the top of her head as she placed it on his chest.

"Most of it, but I needed a break. I'm making tea, and now you are home. We can go and sit down. You can tell me about tonight. Let me finish this, I'll make you some."

Alexander released her so she could make the tea, and walked through to the lounge. He flopped down onto the couch, sinking into the upholstery, and when Anya entered the room he smiled at her. She wore a pair of soft cotton shorts and an oversized pink sweater. Her hair was gathered in a loose, messy bun on top of her head, and when he looked down, he saw pink and grey, candy striped, knee-high socks.

"You look adorable right now, you know?" he said, pulling her hand to his lips when she placed the tea on the table beside him.

Anya sank to the floor beside his legs and unlaced his boots. "I was just comfortable. I didn't think you'd be home so soon…" Her mouth spread into a soft smile when she looked up at him. She removed his shoes, pulled off his black socks and kneeled down to lay her head on his feet.

Alexander sat forward and stroked her hair, then sat back again. "I like it when you look like this, relaxed and happy."

Alexander told her about the initiates, about the flogging with Jonah, and watched her eyes light up when she heard the man's name.

"You genuinely like him don't you?" Alexander asked, and watched her squirm at his feet. "It's okay baby, I don't mind. I want you to help me teach him, and that might mean, at times, getting very intimate, which will be easier if you already share chemistry."

She blushed, but nodded. "I will do as you wish Master."

The memory of the sparks Anya felt at her first contact with Jonah still lingered. It scared her to think of being intimate with someone she felt so strongly attracted to. She cherished her relationship with Alexander, and had no wish to endanger their bond. Though they identified as a polyamorous couple, she had never strayed into that territory. He often played with other submissives, and hadn't, as yet, had a serious secondary relationship, but for her there had always been only him.

Alexander had a gift for reading humans, their moods and emotions. He saw the fear in Anya's eyes, and felt that he could perhaps reaffirm his affection. He reached for her hair, the loosely gathered bun, and pulled her ear to his mouth.

"Enough talking about other men, though. Show your Master how much you missed him."

Anya smiled widely as she unbuttoned his pants and put her mouth to work, sucking his cock. He was already hard under the fabric and, with his hand in her hair, guided her to take all of him into her mouth, down into her throat.

She gagged and placed her hands on his knees, raising herself to change the angle of her neck, taking his length more easily. Alexander groaned; a few stray tears ran down her cheeks, the strain showing on her forehead. He lifted her off him, and gave her time to catch her breath before resuming the act of pulling her soft lips down onto his cock.

"Keep your teeth away from my cock, little one," he grunted.

It didn't take long for him to spill himself deep into her throat, spasms rocking him as the muscles in her throat tightened in her gag reflex. When he released her, she sat back, smiling and wiping the corners of her mouth, where drool had run down her chin.

"Thank you sir, that was fun."

When Anya settled at his feet again, to rest her back against his legs, Alexander pulled her onto the couch beside him. "Don't ever doubt how much I love you, little one. Anya, I will always be here for you, and I will always look after you, understand? You are the most precious thing in my life."

Anya laid her head on his chest and nodded. Shortly after, she was fast asleep. Alexander gathered her into his arms and stood, walking past her study, and her old bedroom, straight to their main bedroom. He tucked her in, went back through the rooms to switch off the lights, stopping to stare into her study for a long while. Then he returned to bed, where he sat down, watching her. She was asleep, and the light wasn't bothering her, so he sat there next to her reading over the information he had received, regarding each new initiate.

After that, he breezed through the financial reports of the club, and lay down in bed. As soon as Anya felt him near her, she sidled over to curl up in his arms.

With a smile Alex fell asleep.

***

On Sunday morning, after sleeping very little the night before, Jonah felt drained, hungover and emotional. He had not had more than one scotch, and a sip of initiation wine, but his stomach felt queasy, and his head ached. Apart from that, his back was bruised, and when he looked in his bathroom mirror after showering, the welts lay thick and evenly spaced across his shoulder blades and down his flanks.

He thought in horror of how he had responded so instinctively to Alexander; the memory of kissing the other man sent his heart pounding and gooseflesh racing down his arms. It was the first time he had done that, and he felt as though he had done something utterly forbidden and taboo. He heard the bells of the Catholic Church two blocks away ringing, and shook his head, pretty sure at that stage that he had a one way ticket to hell.

As these thoughts ran through his head, his phone rang, and he put down the rug he was in the process of rolling up to answer.

"Hi Alex."

Alexander was checking on him. "How are you today, Jonah? I just want to make sure last night was not too much of a mindbender for you."

Jonah exhaled loudly. "I honestly feel a bit fucked up, man. I feel like I have trespassed on every code of manliness out there."

Alex chuckled on the line. "Don't beat yourself up. It is natural to be curious sometimes, and there is nothing wrong with you. And no, I don't think you will go to hell.

I have my own beliefs, I guess, but I think that if you are a good person, a lot can be forgiven."

Jonah frowned to himself. "Why does it feel as though both you and Bartholomew can see inside my head? This is starting, no, not just starting to, it *is* bugging me." He waited for an answer.

"I will discuss that with you when we next meet, but I promise you I am no mind reader. How is your back?"

They discussed a few more things, and then Alexander wished him well for the upcoming move before hanging up. Jonah wasn't sure if the call left him feeling better or worse. It did make him take a mental note, though. He resolved to do the same as Alexander had just done and call, or check on, a play partner after play. He didn't realise that he had just learned one of the most important acts of being a good Dominant.

He continued packing, and within a few hours had all the small things done. He left his kitchen for now, as he still had a week to live in his own place. He resolved to at least go linen shopping during his lunch breaks over the next few days, as his current sheets would in no way fit the beds at his new home.

After he had done everything he could, he sat down with the three photo albums he owned, and removed every picture of Olivia he possessed. He wanted a clean start, and vowed that this move was the beginning of a whole new phase in his life. He burned them, watching the old go up in flames, feeling a lightness in his heart and excitement for the new memories he would make.

Jonah then deleted the pictures off his laptop, and with a happy, contented sigh, went to bed.

Part Two

Chapter 6

Anya passed around the table between Jonah and Alex as she refilled their glasses. This entire dinner experience had so far felt strange to him because they hadn't spent much time together recently. Jonah felt a little removed from the dynamic. Anya was naked tonight, wearing only her brown leather collar and nothing else. She was completely nonplussed by her nudity in front of both him and Alex. Her silky long hair hung in waves down her back, spilling over her shoulders occasionally, and she sat happily at Alex's feet while they ate.

"How is the new house going for you?" Alex asked, lifting his wine glass.

Jonah shrugged and took a deep breath. "I absolutely love it, but I have a lot of work to do. I bought all the décor items and furniture I need, so I am just waiting for a few items to be delivered, then I will get it looking nice and homey. The people who sold to me left most of their things behind, furniture-wise. I was lucky."

He could not help the smile which spread across his face when he thought of the big house he had been living in for two months now. The change had helped him take the first few steps in getting back on his feet after Olivia.

As he sipped the wine he was drawn back to the night of the initiation. "This wine tastes so much like the wine we were given at initiation, but there was something else. too..." He trailed off, looking to Alex.

Alex sat smiling, as did Anya. "I'll tell you the secret: on the night of the initiation you drank a few drops of my blood in your wine, just as I did when Bartholomew initiated me. Your chosen slave or submissive will, one day, when you bond."

"Why would you do that, make people drink your blood?" Jonah frowned.

Alex seemed to think for a moment before he answered. "In our organisation, our club, if you want to call it that, the power of the collective group comes from the bond we share. Bartholomew has amazing abilities which passed to those of us he chose when we partook. This might just be a placebo effect, but people believe. His abilities don't come to us in their full strength, but enhance our own natural abilities, once we find them."

Jonah still had so many questions, and for the life of him he could not figure out why the blood thing didn't freak him out any more. And what was Bartholomew? Nobody had taken the time to explain the mysterious man to him.

He had been so busy with his move and work over the past few weeks, he had not spent extended periods of time with Alex and Anya. He was reminded of this every time Anya brushed past him, or Alex turned his smile on him.

For now, he was fixated on the idea of powers. "What abilities, Alex? This is beginning to sound a bit like a fantasy story I haven't read the prologue or introduction to."

Alex chuckled when he answered. "Bartholomew can read minds. I am pretty sure you figured that out at your first meeting. I have a way of seeing people in need of help, something Anya and I share. That is why she does the work she does. If you two would excuse me, I want to check that my dungeon is ready; we are going to do some learning after this." He stood to leave.

Jonah glanced at Anya. "What do you do when you are not kneeling to him?" he asked, curiously, narrowing his eyes.

She brushed hair from her face. "I have my own psychology practice."

This caught Jonah off-guard. "You? You own a business, and yet choose to do this?" He gestured to her position and to the collar. "I am sorry. I don't understand."

"Jonah, to me, my submission comes out of great love for Alex. Our story is a complicated and long one, but it's not just that. I am responsible and in charge of other people all day, and it is tiring. Being Dominant is not the strongest part of my natural personality. I crave the release from making decisions, and that is what Alex gives me. With him I can relax and know that I am taken care of, while knowing he still respects me as an individual."

Jonah sat staring at her as though a light bulb had just turned on in his head. "I kind of think I get that, I mean, after the flogging with Alex, that is. Oh man, I can totally see the appeal to submit."

Anya smiled from where she sat on the floor. "I know, and I can see you have more questions. Feel free to ask me anything. I can answer you now."

Jonah rubbed his face with both hands. "Okay, why is there a symbol of a chalice on everything? And why is everything purple?"

He wanted to carry on, but she held up a hand to silence him. "One thing at a time, honey. The chalice is in part representative of the Realm's version of a Holy Grail, you could say; the blood we share when we join The Forgotten Realm. It is also literal, The Realm owns a relic, an ancient silver chalice from the time of the Crusades which Bartholomew apparently brought to the very first meeting. It has not been changed or replaced, ever. It is shared, and it joins us together. Each Master has his own replica made of pure silver. The original remains on display at the club. As to the purple, it is a colour of royalty and symbolises the hierarchy and respect we hold for the Masters, The Realm and for each other."

Alexander re-entered the room, taking his seat. "Everything is ready." He looked from Anya to Jonah. "You guys having a Q and A?"

They nodded simultaneously, and Jonah spoke. "Why the robes? It seems a little medieval, doesn't it?" He felt as though a million questions were popping to the surface now, and he could finally get answers for them.

Alex took this one, and as he sat running his fingers through Anya's hair, her eyes closed with the pleasure of the sensation. "The robes distinguish the initiated from the uninitiated. The slaves garb is flattering to the women who are such, plus, it adds a touch of drama. Who doesn't enjoy the act of dressing up and looking different for a night? It affects ones mood. The robes basically add a bit of the theatrical." He spread his arms like a master of ceremonies. "It all makes us feel unique in the continuous daily waves of dull and mundane humanity. Shall we go and play with some ropes, among other things?" He stood suddenly, casting a glance at Anya. "All this talk of robes and moods and drama…"

Jonah watched as Alex stretched, the edge of his shirt lifting to show toned abs. Anya stood gracefully, and both she and Jonah followed Alex toward the dungeon.

As they entered what Alex referred to as a 'dungeon', Jonah wiped his eyes to look again, then stood surveying the room. He had not expected what was in front of him. He stood in a brightly lit room with gleaming white walls, shining and sterile-clean. A set of chains swung from the ceiling in the centre of the room, and against the far wall a white leather sofa looked very comfortable. He remembered the chains in his own dungeon and smiled; they seemed to be a common accessory.

The set of stocks off to one side were painted black, and contrasted with the general light of the room. Alex laughed when he saw Jonah's face, and leaned against the white-upholstered cross fixed to the wall nearest him.

"Surprised it's not medieval, dark, dank and scary?" he asked.

Jonah exhaled loudly. "I thought you couldn't read minds? It might not be dark, but this brightness and all the white is unnerving. You've opened a whole new level of scary. It makes me think of insane asylum themed horror movies."

Anya giggled and Jonah turned to look at her, standing so comfortably in this environment. Alex approached her and planted a soft kiss on her forehead. Jonah's heart melted a little at the tender interaction, Anya's eyes closing to let soft lashes fluttering. Jonah couldn't help but think again how beautiful she was, whether dressed up or naked and without any makeup, as she was tonight.

Alex walked to a built in cupboard and swung the doors wide, picked out a rope, a set of wrist cuffs and a gift bag that sat on one of the shelves. He placed the ropes and cuffs on the floor near the chains. The gift bag he handed to Jonah.

"I loved your response to the flogging so much, both watching it as well as being flogged yourself, that I had to get you this…"

Jonah gingerly opened the bag and lifted out the item in it. "Oh my God, Alex, this is beautiful," he exclaimed, holding the flogger he'd lifted from the bag.

The handle was elaborately carved oak, and the actual whip was made of heavy, deep purple suede. Jonah let the strands fall to the ground, and shivered at the sound of them hitting the floor. The memory of being flogged by Alex, and that which followed the encounter, would not soon fade from his memory. Jonah looked down to see the whip strands brush the floor, and smiled at the sight of the dark purple against the black of the interlocking rubber floor tiles.

"Thank you so much. I love it."

Alex moved Anya, his hand in the small of her back, and positioned her under the dangling chains. "Let's show you how to use it, then."

Alex picked up the set of cuffs and fastened them around Anya's wrists as she held them out in front of her, one at a time. He then lifted them and linked the cuffs to the chains overhead. Then he stepped back, away from her stretched out body.

Jonah's breath caught in his throat at the sight. Anya's feet were flat on the ground, but she stood tightly stretched, her back arched and head thrown back. Her skin glowed alabaster smooth, and her hair shone in the bright light. Jonah jumped a little when the lights dimmed; Alex had turned a switch near the door. When he glanced back at Anya all Jonah could focus on was the curve of her behind, flowing smoothly to long, shapely legs.

Alex started talking again, and as he did, he went to stand in front of Anya, placing her between them. He brushed her hair forward over her shoulder.

"With flogging, you want to be careful not to hit her in the face with strands that get a little out of control. Always instruct your submissive to keep their face down and forward." Alex positioned her head before he moved to run his hands down her shoulder blades and back. "The best places to focus on are the shoulders, over the hips and down to the thighs. Just try to avoid the kidney area. Anya is quite slim and hasn't got much padding over that part of her back. At the front of the body, you can flog the breasts and over the thighs, just again, be careful of the face and try to avoid the stomach with particularly hard impacts."

Alex smiled at the sight of Jonah's obvious nervousness when he nodded and mouthed, "Okay." The man's hands were shaking and he seemed to be biting his tongue.

Alex strode toward the cupboard again, and returned to Jonah and Anya with a black, dry-wipe marker. "Take this and mark the areas on her skin I just told you are okay to flog. Make patches or stripes, however you wish."

Jonah took the marker from Alex and shook his head. The thought that he was touching Anya, a naked woman he truly desired, blew his mind. He closed his eyes and took a deep breath to steady his hands. When he cautiously approached Anya, she hung in the restraints, an eyebrow raised and a cheeky smile on her face.

"Come on Mr., I can't exactly bite…"

Jonah chuckled and stooped to draw on her, while Alex sat on the couch with his arms folded across his chest, watching. When Jonah drew the marker across Anya's ribs a fit of giggles escaped her, and she raised a small foot, cringing away from the touch.

"Oh, you're ticklish, are you? So, you can't bite but you can squirm?" Jonah stood back. "All I would have to do to torment you is to continue."

He worked his way farther down her ribs, moving across her back and eventually down toward her thighs, while she hung, wriggling and squirming, in the restraints.

By the time he finished, Anya was gasping and a thin film of sweat beaded her brow from the laughter.

Alex walked up behind her and wrapped his arms around her. "That was fun to watch, pet, you giggle so prettily. I don't think Jonah imagined BDSM having giggles involved." He kissed her shoulder before he picked up Jonah's new flogger. "Come and watch, Jonah, I will demonstrate once, and then she is all yours."

Alex measured his distance from Anya by swinging the flogger and watching the strands graze her skin. Her little flinches set a smile on his face before he found his rhythm. Alex noticed how Jonah stood slightly off to the side, making sure he wouldn't get in the way.

"Good on you for keeping a space between you and the backswing. If you walk into a whip wielded by someone else in public, it is your fault for getting smacked in the face, not theirs." Alex dropped his arm after roughly five minutes and beckoned Jonah closer. "You see where the marks lie, along where you drew on her skin?"

Jonah nodded, reaching for her back and running his index finger along a red and raised welt. "It's beautiful."

Anya exhaled as he touched her. Her face was leaning against her raised arm and Jonah felt incredibly drawn to touch her face. He couldn't resist the urge. He walked around her and raised her chin. "Are you okay? Will you cope with me doing that, too?"

"Jonah, I can take anything my Master throws at me. He has explained safe words to you?" When he nodded she continued. "Then you know that if I am, at any point not okay, I will use either a warning word or a safe word. Don't constantly ask me if I am okay, it kills my buzz." She dropped her head, and while Alex chuckled in the background, Jonah moved to stand behind her.

"Okay, I won't ask again. I am just nervous about hurting you." Jonah took the flogger Alex handed to him.

"Just find the correct distance from her, and remember to untangle the strands on roughly every alternate backswing." With that last advice, Alex returned to his seat on the couch to watch from a safe distance as Jonah slowly swung the flogger.

It took a few mislaid strikes, accompanied by flinches from Anya and awkward apologies from Jonah, but he found his movement, combing his fingers through the leather on the backswings and laying a smooth set of welts across the backs of Anya's thighs. He felt himself get hard at the sight of her body moving with the impacts and the little grunts that escaped her periodically. When he stopped he was breathing hard and he flexed his shoulder.

"This is hard work."

Alex went straight to Anya, who was, by now, looking slightly limp in the chains and cuffs. He scraped his nails over her abused skin and lifted her head, smiling at the glazed look in her eyes. "I think somebody is ready to cum for me, aren't you baby?"

Alex's mouth was in her neck, his body pressed tightly to hers. Jonah felt that he was intruding on a very private moment and didn't quite know where to look. He started moving away, his eyes everywhere except on the couple in front of him. He realised then, that in his own life an 'open' relationship like this would never work, not if this felt so awkward when it had the full consent of all present.

"Jonah, come here," Alex said. "I think this little thing needs a bit of distraction while I fetch her favourite vibrator." He beckoned for Jonah to take his place and then went to his trusty cupboard.

Standing in front of Anya, Jonah could hardly breathe when she put her head on his shoulder, nuzzling his neck. He stepped closer to her, feeling her hot skin right through his clothing, and he instinctively reached his arms around her, running his flat palms down her back and cupping her arse. The flesh sat firmly in his hands, and when he squeezed the round orbs she moaned softly against his chest, raised herself onto her toes and hollowed her back to get more physical contact from his legs. He couldn't think straight; being this intimate with her was torment of the worst kind.

The crux of his discomfort was the erection building between their bodies, and he felt himself blushing. He needed to do something about his feelings for her, and soon. Jonah wished at that moment he could read her mind, to tell whether she felt as strongly about him, too, or if her reaction was purely a by-product of subspace.

He heard Alex's footsteps draw closer and disentangled himself from Anya. The longing in her eyes at his moving away did not go unnoticed by Alex. While Jonah took his turn on the couch, Alex kicked Anya's feet apart and with one hand on her throat, spread the lips of her sex and placed the head of a Hitachi vibrator against her clit.

Anya squirmed in his grasp. "No, no, no, please, not in front of him, please sir." She begged and pleaded in his hands, twisting her head from side to side.

Alex shook his head. "No, no, no? If I tell you to cum for me, you will fucking cum, pet. Simple."

Alex ground the vibrator against her, clutching her firmly, and then he kissed her. His movements were forceful, and Jonah saw the wetness from her sex glisten on the Hitachi as she clenched every muscle in her body. Her breath was coming in short gasps, and when she came, liquid ran down her thighs. Jonah took a deep breath and adjusted his pants to accommodate his hard-on. He ran his hands through his hair and exhaled loudly, aroused beyond anything he'd experienced.

He watched Alex un-cuff Anya and let her settle down on the floor to relax. She rubbed her own arms to get circulation back to her fingers. They were clearly a bit sore from being raised for so long. "Thank you sir."

Her voice was soft, and Alex petted her head affectionately. "Anya, clean and tidy this room, and when you are done, put on something comfortable, baby, then join us in the living room. You can make some coffee for all of us, does that sound good?"

At this instruction, Anya nodded and Alex led Jonah from the room.

Jonah felt relief wash over him when Alex was the first to broach the subject. "What makes you uncomfortable here, Jonah? I am going to guess it involves being intimate with Anya because she is mine." He sat down on the large sofa, resting his elbows on his knees while Jonah took the armchair.

"I have a history of straight monogamy, Alex. It feels like I am violating your relationship by being so... I don't know, physical with Anya. I am not used to this, and I know it's how things seem to be in your life. Just give me some time to adjust. So much has changed in my life recently. I really just need to find a bit of calm in the chaos." It felt as though he had said everything in one breath, and he was overwhelmed.

Just as he got this load off his chest, Anya entered the room carrying a tray with a French press of coffee and three cups and saucers. She gracefully knelt in front of Alex to allow him to fix his cup, and then repeated the procedure in front of Jonah, glancing furtively at him, an unreadable expression in those deep, green eyes. She seemed to have put on a mask.

Only once they had prepared their coffee did she set the tray on the coffee table and make a cup for herself. She never positioned her back toward either of them, and constantly watched them for signs of displeasure, especially Alex. To Jonah, it seemed as though her entire life and every action were to please Alex. It mystified and attracted him deeply, yet also left him wondering about how happy someone could truly be living like this.

He wanted to know more, and was sure Alex would explain. "How do you cope with watching her be touched by another? Aren't you jealous?" he asked, taking a sip of his coffee.

"There is a deep-seated trust between Anya and I, we have a very long history. She has lived with me since she was eighteen, and over the years our relationship eventually grew into that of Master and slave. It was not immediate, nor was it sexual at first. Anya had many past issues to deal with before I would let her into my bed, regardless of the fact that there was strong chemistry. I wanted her to know she could trust me beyond sex. Without the expectation of physical intimacy, relationships develop stronger foundations, and BDSM gave us so much to work with, without the pressure of sex." He spoke of her as if she were not there, but she didn't seem to mind, she had replaced her cup on the table and was leaning against his legs, dressed in a fluffy sweatshirt and pink panties. She had washed the markings off her skin.

"We opened our relationship to others because of the activities we enjoy. I like playing with other submissives, and I teach new initiates, within both the club, which we refer to as The Realm, and privately. I was not designed to be monogamous, and now, instead of cheating, I am open with Anya about everything I do. She also has the same freedom to explore, but has not found an appropriate person to do so with as yet." He drained his cup and handed it to Anya. "Take that to the kitchen please, pet."

Alex waited for her to leave the room. "I think she likes you a lot, Jonah, I see chemistry between you two. I have already mentioned that she will assist with your instruction, but I want you to know I am happy for a close bond to build between you, and I think it will happen easily. There's something between you. It helps build trust and makes play more intense."

Anya returned and took her position at Alex's feet once again. She looked utterly exhausted, and Jonah needed the cue to leave. His head spun with all that he had felt, seen and heard already, and he needed thinking space.

"Thank you both for a wonderful evening, I have thoroughly enjoyed myself and indeed learned a lot. Alex, thank you for my flogger, it is beyond beautiful. I wish you both a good night, it is late and I have to work tomorrow. Perhaps we can incorporate rope into our next lesson? And I will think about the whole play thing, I need to wrap my head around it."

With this he stood and reached to shake Alex's hand, walking behind him as he escorted Jonah to the door.

"You have a lot to think about, but yes, rope indeed. Next time," Alex said as they stood at the door. "Don't hesitate to call if you have questions, okay?"

Jonah nodded and made his way to his car, got in and drove home. He was still getting used to the idea of the mansion being his own. The whole sales process, both of his apartment and the mansion, had simply been too easy thanks to Bartholomew's interference. Even getting the mortgage he'd needed to cover the excess of the mansion's cost had come without complications, and covered his furnishing requirements easily. He didn't trust anything in life to go so smoothly, and felt like he was going to be hit by some terrible misfortune soon. As for what the misfortune would be, he could not guess.

***

Jonah parked in one of the three double garages under the house and got out of his car. When he saw all the empty space he got excited about the potential it held. He could not afford to fill it with cars, so now he had a workspace he could do something with. Due to the busy and very much dull routine of his life up to now, Jonah had never had a hobby besides reading, and the library upstairs now held his boxes of books yet to be unpacked onto the beautiful shelves.

He walked through the garage to the stairs leading into the kitchen, saying "Hellooooooo" and listening to it echo. He laughed at how easily amused he was, still enjoying things he used to as a child. Too many adults lost the ability to do that. While he stood on the stairs he thought about the reading he'd done on things like pet play, and little or daddy dominant interaction. All of it sounded like so much fun, playful fun.

He would think of something to do with the extra space in time, when he had a budget to do so again. As he was about to put the usage of it out of his mind the perfect brainwave struck him, hard. He stopped on the first step to look back. The house didn't have a hot tub, fancy as it was.

That was it, he mused, standing there stroking his chin. He would use this area, rebuilding it a little, as an alternate entertainment area, and add a nice hot tub and downstairs bar. That would work, and he could more than likely do the alterations himself. With a nod he continued up the stairs and pushed open the door into the kitchen. Yes, it could be his man-cave. Jonah walked to the fridge and pulled out a bottle of wine, pouring a glass to take with him into the library, where he planned to do some unpacking.

He clambered over the boxes scattered about and stared again at the desk and chair. The owners of the house had left behind a number of large items, along with a note for Jonah when he first entered the house, wishing him all the best for the future as well as congratulating him on his initiation.

His parents had taught him to be wary of too much good at once, setting up his discomfort about good fortune, and to guard himself against misfortune, both in life and love. His mother had come over to help him pack before he left his apartment, and he smiled as he removed a photo album from a box she must have sneaked in. It was filled with pictures of his childhood friends, family and memories of their holidays. He set it on the edge of the desk, to page through at some point. The pillow from the box he placed on the corner armchair, and the throw he hung over the footstool. It was starting to feel a bit more like home, having a few of his own things around him, as opposed to constantly looking at new things everywhere he turned.

It was almost four in the morning when Jonah climbed the stairs to his bedroom, exhausted. The stairwell walls were bereft of picture frames, but he planned to rectify that. He loved art, and preferred it on the walls to personal family pictures, especially in the dating phase of his life. He enjoyed keeping things private until he knew a girl had the potential to be a long term partner. The only picture he had placed so far was one of his parents, and it stood in a frame in the living room.

Jonah placed the flogger Alex had given him on the dresser, planning to do some work in the dungeon the next day He stripped as he walked to the bathroom. A shower rendered him fresh, and he prepped his gym bag for the following afternoon's session with Blaine. The subject of the club still hadn't come up with him, although Jonah held onto the possibility that Blaine was a member, too. That would be an interesting talk, no doubt. He fell asleep, folding himself into the dark blue bedding he had bought for this room: Egyptian cotton, from the fitted sheets to the duvet. It was a heavenly, comfortable bed and he looked forward to having a woman in it.

Jonah's dreams were filled with erotic visions. He kept seeing Alex's dungeon, and Anya hanging on the chains. In his dream he was alone with her, and after flogging her he had fucked her while she was still tied. It was so vivid and so real he woke with a start, and his erection raised the duvet, he was so hard and desperate for release.

"Fuck this!"

He got out of bed cursing his lust for Anya, and got dressed to go to his gym, one of the rooms he had not seen on his initial tour.

It was seven a.m., and Jonah had barely slept three hours, yet he'd spent thirty minutes running as hard as he could on the treadmill, trying to work off his frustration before heading to the office.

Now that he was in a very residential suburb and far from the public transport system, he drove to and from work, and had been getting admiring glances from several of the office PAs. They were materialistic girls and didn't appeal to him, and the glances were only happening because nobody had thought he owned a car, and were now beginning to wonder what else they perhaps didn't know about him. At the office he kept very much to himself, not really counting any of his colleagues as friends.

***

A cream coloured envelope sat waiting for Jonah on his desk as he walked into his office. It leaned almost casually against the keyboard of his PC. To Jonah it spelled something to do with The Realm, he knew instantly. His suspicions were confirmed when he picked it up and opened it to find a single card with elegant, yet playful, handwriting on it.

Jonah,
Bartholomew instructed me to come to you tonight, he feels that you are in need of… Well, let's say, some fun.
I will be at your house at seven, and I will bring everything to prepare your dinner.
Yours in service,
Alice

He stared at it in disbelief and placed it back in the envelope before he sat down to boot up his PC. He had emails to check and clients to deal with. On top of that he was so tired he could barely think; he was simply grateful it was Friday. He put the envelope aside. He was tired and disappointed he wouldn't have an early night to crash and sleep, and sat moodily reading through his emails.

At lunch time he grabbed a sandwich from the canteen downstairs and went straight back to work. He ignored the lascivious smile Stavros cast at him on a coffee break, and ploughed through his paperwork as efficiently as he could. His MMA training started at five thirty and ended at six thirty, and when he left the office at five, Stavros stood against a nearby doorpost with his arms crossed over his chest.

"Have a good evening MacPherson."

Jonah didn't like the sarcastic tone of his voice, but maintained politeness. "And you!" he called, striding into a nearby elevator to go down to the parking garage. He frowned to himself. He'd left the card from Alice on his desk, and it had been missing after his lunch break.

At least it had contained nothing graphic. He chided himself for the irresponsibility and swore to be more careful. It took minutes to arrive at the gym, and as he walked into the matted area after changing, Jonah stopped dead in his tracks.

On the mat, caught in a headlock with Blaine's thighs around her neck, was the red-haired slave from the initiation night. Jonah would recognise her hair anywhere.

The girl struggled savagely while Jonah watched from the door, thinking his suspicions about Blaine were confirmed. He cleared his throat, and with comedic ease Blaine looked up, completely ignoring the struggling girl under him.

"Oh hi Jonah, just give me a minute, will you?" Blaine changed his position, kissed the girl on the forehead and then released her. "Come meet Jonah, he is new to our club."

They approached Jonah, with her looking decidedly dishevelled in black gym gear beside Blaine, who seemed as relaxed as ever. "Jonah, this is Persephone, she is my... Well, she is mine."

Jonah smiled at her. "Hi again, you brought drinks to Alex and I on the night of my, you know..." He didn't feel comfortable discussing these things in such a public space.

"Oh yes! Hi Jonah." Her voice had a sweet innocence to it and she inclined her head politely. Persephone turned to Blaine. "May I please go and shower, sir?"

He dismissed her, and he and Jonah were left alone.

"I knew it!" Jonah exclaimed the moment the girl was gone. "I was so convinced I'd seen you, but I denied it to myself."

Blaine merely chuckled and walked to the middle of the floor while Jonah put his bag down. They slowly started warming up, running a few sprints and easing into basic stretches. Blaine worked him through grappling and throws and left Jonah feeling beaten up. When they finished and stood with their hands on their knees, breathing hard, Jonah spoke again, a little frustrated that Blaine hadn't said more about the club or Persephone.

"I'd love it if you two came to dinner sometime, to hear about how you found each other? My new house is perfect for entertaining."

Blaine nodded. "I like that idea. Why don't you speak to Bartholomew or Alex, or even just do some research, and host a proper high-protocol dinner, something for our kind of people to enjoy? I reckon you'll like the idea."

Jonah had no idea what he meant, but would start by asking Alice later, while she cooked for him. "I will have to ask and do some research, but when I get it together I will let you know."

Blaine smacked him on the shoulder. "Good man, I think you are going to enjoy this journey you've embarked on. Not to be cheesy or anything, but it changes your life."

Jonah straightened up from his bent over position. "It already has."

It was six forty-five by the time he pulled into his drive, parked the car and sprinted to the shower. He dressed in comfortable, scuffed jeans and a light blue, button down shirt with the sleeves rolled up to just below the elbows. He spritzed on cologne and made his way downstairs. Jonah eyed the dining room; the large round table had been left behind by the owners, but he had bought the eight ornate wooden chairs that now surrounded it.

A deep red tablecloth covered the wood, and blended beautifully with the wood-panelled walls to give the room an old feel. It looked reminiscent of the house in the Underworld movies. Plush, expensive.

"And inhabited by vampires…" He said to himself, and walked away laughing. He had filled the wall cabinet with a white dinner set, and the crystal wine glasses his mother had given to him while he was still dating Olivia. Along with these things, he had a set of antique silverware he had found in a pawn shop for a fraction of the original cost, and placemats in a deep red colour from the home-décor shop he had found his other things at. He could host a formal dinner here, he just needed to know what was involved in a 'high-protocol' dinner.

Jonah stood in the doorway when his gate buzzer rang. The sound made him jump. He pressed the button on the intercom and answered.

"Hello?"

The reply was quick, cheerful, and definitely Alice. "Hi Jonah! It's me, your servant for the evening."

He heard her giggling as he buzzed the gate to open, then made his way to the front door to let her in. He stood waiting as a white VW Beetle pulled up to the parking area, and then went to help her carry her grocery bags.

Alice had brought everything from salad to fresh bread, ready-made soup and even wine. She chatted as they walked back toward the door. "I thought I'd bring a light meal just in case you wanted to play, it's not so much fun on a full stomach. And I brought a bottle of really nice white wine…"

He lost track for a moment, nervous at the thought of play. What would he do with her? How would he…

"Jonah? You still with me?" she piped up, touching his shoulder lightly.

"Um, yes. Sorry, I zoned out for a moment there." He turned to put the bags down on the counter and watched her manoeuvre with ease around the kitchen, finding pots and setting out wine glasses.

"Where is your opener?" She held up the wine.

He reached into a nearby drawer and handed it to her. "There we go."

Alice poured two glasses of wine, handed him one and looked him dead in the eye. "Jonah, Bartholomew wants me to serve you tonight. He was quite detailed, and sent you a gift which I will give to you shortly."

Jonah swallowed a mouthful of his chilled wine. "Can you please clarify what you mean by serve?" His voice sounded hoarse.

She smiled. "Sure. It means I will prepare your dinner. I will do that dressed as you wish me to be, or undressed. A lot of Dom's like nudity, it signifies trust and a willingness to be vulnerable. I will rub your feet if you desire, you can take me to your dungeon, if you want. I am your toy tonight and you can do whatever you wish, within boundaries of course. Like no slapping my face. Oh, and I am to serve your sexual needs, too, if you want. I'm just saying it out loud because I don't think you are the kind of guy who would just assume these things." Alice blushed when she said this.

Jonah's jaw dropped. "Wow. I might need a moment to get used to that idea. Why would I slap you? That's terrible…" He sat down on a chair at the kitchen table.

Alice shrugged. "Um, some Dominants enjoy doing that, but I have an eye problem and it can do serious damage, so, hard limit. I like you, you're hot. And we are both single, so I don't see any problem with us having sex. Plus, pretend I am your submissive. Practice. You will get some confidence, I swear, I can even give you pointers and if this doesn't lead to sex, I am fine with that. No harm no foul. I am here for your pleasure tonight."

Jonah stopped her when she turned toward the counter to start preparing dinner. "Wait, what are you wearing under your dress?" he asked. It felt indecent, but good, to ask a woman something like this.

Alice glanced down at her black satin wrap dress and smiled. "I wore lacy undies, and they're black, with hold-up stockings."

With his heart thundering in his throat Jonah made the decision to let go and see where the night went. "I want you to take off your dress for me, Alice. Keep everything else on. The shoes stay, too."

He folded his arms and stroked his chin as he watched her untie the dress, slip it off her shoulders and neatly fold it to hang it over a chair. She proceeded to move with the utmost grace to prepare dinner.

"Alice, what do you know about high-protocol dinners?" Jonah followed her movements: she was not a tall girl but had the right proportional curves to look good.

She answered with an expectant glance. "Oh! They are dinners where the slaves or submissives serve their Master's every need. You get instructed to behave a certain way, and it's all very posh, except the slaves are usually naked or wearing body jewellery only. Anya knows a lot more than I do, I think she and Alex do the high-protocol type stuff."

Jonah thought about this while his gaze lingered on her. Her bra, sheer lace, which looked frighteningly expensive, didn't have much to it. Her nipples pressed against the minimal fabric and her breasts moved as she breathed; they were round and firm. His gaze drifted down the length of her body, to a cinched waist which blossomed into a firm-looking derriere and shapely legs. They held muscle memories of sport, Jonah guessed.

As he sat there being entertained by her, he realised he felt physical attraction to this girl, but no desire to get to know her particularly well, questioning her about sports in school, for example. The realisation made him feel like he was being an arsehole. He wasn't the use-and-discard sort. His desire for Anya, in contrast, was a thing of depth he wasn't entirely sure he grasped. He wanted to know everything about that woman, down to the past Alex had hinted at.

Jonah forcefully pulled himself back to the present, and thanked Alice as she refilled his wine and put a platter of mozzarella, fresh basil and sliced tomato in the middle of the table, returning to fetch sliced fresh bread spread with creamy butter.

"Dig in, Mr. MacPherson. Where shall I sit to eat?"

Jonah thought for a moment while she waited with her hands clasped in front of her.

"Sit here, kneel next to me and I will feed you." He pointed at the ground near his legs.

Alice obeyed with a smile, sinking down into a kneeling position, patiently waiting. Her satin-soft lips brushed his fingers as Jonah fed her a morsel of cheese with basil, and she licked his fingers clean when tomato juice ran down them.

"You have very nice hands, Jonah, sir," she said softly when he held her wine glass for her to drink.

Jonah was caught off-guard by her addressing him with the title, barely managing to keep his composure. He stroked her chin to disguise the tremble in his hand. "Thank you, Alice."

When the salad was gone, Alice stood in one smooth movement to clear the table and warm the creamy tomato soup she had brought. Jonah watched her move again, the muscles shifting under skin, the grace with which her limbs flowed.

"Alice, why is there a specific way all the submissives I have seen at the club move and walk?"

"We are taught how to move in a way which is pleasing to the eye, to walk with grace and sit, stand and kneel in specific ways. Our eventual owners and long term partners can teach us their own way, but to serve at The Realm, the more experienced women teach the new ones." She continued stirring soup while she spoke. "It must be nice to be able to get the answers to all your questions now, as opposed to when Anya brought you the first time? I remember the feeling well myself."

Jonah nodded. "You have no idea. Well, I suppose you do, as you say. Sorry, I am blabbering nonsense."

Alice brought their bowls of soup along with more freshly sliced bread and settled at his feet again. This time Jonah handed her bowl to her. "I don't think this would be ideal to feed you, you'd end up covered in food."

With a giggle she ate her dinner, both of them silent.

They finished eating and Jonah stood after Alice had cleared the table. "Leave the dishes," he said, when he saw her head toward the scullery.

Alice stopped, and then she jumped on the spot. "Oh! Bartholomew sent an early Christmas present for you! Well, I call it that because it is a huge set of toys for your dungeon." She skipped toward the bags she had carried in. "He said it was a 'dungeon warming' gift."

"I have not once ceased to be amazed by the kindness and generosity of the club toward me, a total stranger. You know they orchestrated the sale of my apartment when I wanted to buy this house?"

He was shocked again when she answered: "I know the agent who sold it. She isn't one of us, but she's a good woman. And they do this for people they want, who might have a future they don't see themselves."

Jonah led Alice through to his living room with her still holding the bag in her arms. He sat down in an armchair and watched as she set the bag down and naturally settled herself on the fluffy carpet.

"I like what you've done with this room." She sat looking around her. "I can't believe they left so much furniture. This is beautiful stuff."

"I, for one, am not complaining." Jonah loved the deep blue of the furnishings. The coffee table he had bought, as the owners had not left one behind. His choice was a square mahogany table, solid and strong, and now that he thought about it, the perfect height to bend a girl over and… He shook his head. "Yup, no complaints. Let's see what's in this bag, shall we?" He gestured toward it and Alice moved it closer for him to unpack.

He decided to blindly reach in and pull one item out at a time, his first being a set of four adjustable leather cuffs. "Nice."

Alice made appreciative sounds from the floor. Jonah pulled out a neatly coiled rope, and then another.

"Natural fibre," Alice said, reaching out to touch it. "This is expensive stuff."

The texture felt rough against Jonah's hands. "Doesn't this hurt your skin?" He fondled the rope.

Alice shook her head. "Nope."

With a shrug Jonah reached in again, lifting out a big, rectangular black box.

At this, Alice squeaked, "Oh my God. He gave you a wand!"

Jonah recognised the vibrator Alex had used on Anya and smiled. "So, this is good, then?" He raised an eyebrow at her.

Alice squirmed before she nodded excitedly. "The best! Oh! This one is cordless and rechargeable!"

Jonah placed it next to the chair and again reached into the bag. A very normal pack of condoms. "Safety first." He chuckled.

There was a hairbrush, which he smiled at, and a length of silk, which Alice cleared up for him when he frowned. "Blindfold," she said.

When he pulled out the final item Alice wrapped her arms swiftly around her torso, covering her breasts. "Just for the record, Jonah, those don't come near me."

"What are these?" He turned the small metal items from side to side.

Alice's brow furrowed. "You really know nothing, don't you? Sorry! I didn't mean to sound condescending. They are vicious nipple clamps, called Clover clamps, and for me, hard, very much hard, limit."

Jonah's lack of knowledge scared him, and he had to admit this. "I have not read about, or discussed, what limits are. I have a basic idea, but need to talk to Alex. As for the toys, I'll get the hang of what I like." He looked at the pile of goodies and picked up the brush, smacking his own palm with it. "Of all of this awesome and intriguing stuff, I feel like using this. I think you should go bend your pretty little self over the coffee table."

Jonah used the hairbrush to direct her to the side, which would leave him staring directly at her arse. He quite wickedly waited for Alice to drape herself over the table first, and then spoke. "Oh, and I think you should lose the panties."

He watched as she awkwardly raised herself, stood, and shyly slipped off her underwear. He could clearly see the damp patch on them from where he sat. "Hand me those, please."

He held the delicate lace in his hand as he watched her resume her bent over position, the underwear in his hand warm from her body and scented with her arousal.

Her sex peeked out from the juncture of her thighs, glistening, engorged and rosy pink, free of hair. Jonah walked around her and silently enjoyed the nervousness building in her eyes, and the trembling of her body. Here, in front of him, was a beautiful woman, bent over his table, nervous and aroused, still wearing her stockings and stilettos, toes gracefully pointed. The black lace of her bra served to accentuate how pale she was. He liked that she had no tattoos or piercings he could see, just soft, pale skin.

"Alice, do you think you'll scream if I hit you with this hairbrush?" He smacked his palm again, watching her jump a little at the sound.

She turned her face toward him and nodded. "I think so, sir."

He sighed, having fun. "I will have to dull the sound somehow. I am not a fan of loud noises. Hmm, now I wonder how I could mute your screams..." He squatted down beside her. "Open your mouth."

When she did so, he stuffed her panties into it. Her eyes widened in surprise; she had clearly not expected that. Jonah reached for the silk scarf from the bag and used it to tie his makeshift gag in place.

He stood back to admire the sight, and then walked a slow deliberate circle around her and the table. He smugly noticed the coffee table was indeed the perfect height for taking a girl from behind in this position. Alice followed him with her eyes, wary, as he knelt beside her. He raised the brush to inspect it fully within her view, as her eyes nervously kept track of his every movement.

"This does look as though it might hurt," he murmured, suppressing his chuckles as she muttered something through the cloth in her mouth.

He smacked her quite gently the first time, getting his bearings, and saw her body shake with giggles, the laughter obvious in her shining eyes.

Jonah smirked. "What? Wasn't that hard enough?"

The next swing was not a soft one, and nor were any of the ones that followed. He spread the attack over both cheeks until they were good and pink, progressively hitting harder and harder. When Jonah glanced at her face all traces of laughter were long gone; she squeezed her eyes shut and a single, mascara stained tear ran from them.

Jonah turned the brush over in his hand and ran the rough bristles across her skin, over the edges of her arse and the brightest imprints left by the tool. His cock hardened in his jeans as gooseflesh rose across Alice's back and she moaned softly.

Kneeling behind her, he reached for the scarf around her head and untied it. She spat out the panties, while her breath came in short pants.

"Alice, you are here willingly, and you said that your presence was to serve my needs, also sexually. Are you still okay with that? I don't ask out of weakness, but I am big on consent."

When she nodded to affirm her tearfully uttered 'yes', Jonah reached for her hands, pulling them together to hold on top of her back.

"Keep your hands here," he instructed, unbuttoning his jeans to slip them down and release his erection. He reached for the condoms which lay on top of the bag's contents and tore the package open. While he rolled one on, he stroked her arse cheeks alternately and watched her tremble in anticipation. Jonah grasped her small wrists in one hand and slipped easily into her slick sex, feeling himself fill her completely as she tilted her hips to take him in.

An involuntary groan escaped him as her warmth enveloped him, and something animalistic inside took over. He tangled his fingers in her hair and with a groan started pounding savagely into her. He felt the soft cushioning of her body against the solid table, and found himself not caring whether it hurt or bruised her. Only his release mattered. Under him, she curled her fingers around his hand, holding on tightly, and he saw her bite her lip as she braced herself, the mass of her blonde hair escaping to cover her face.

Jonah closed his eyes and saw Anya under him, her skin golden against his own, and with the illusion of her in his mind, his orgasm shook him.

Alice stayed draped over the table, breathing hard, as he wiped sweat from his brow and exclaimed, "Fuck. That was fun."

Jonah cleaned up, wrapping the discarded condom in tissue, and buttoned his jeans. Alice straightened from her position and brushed the hair from her face.

"Well, that was creative," she commented, red faced.

"I'll take that as a compliment. Just relax here, I will fetch us some water. I am sure you need it."

He left the room, running a hand through his hair when he got to the kitchen. He had never just fucked a girl without an emotional connection, and the sensation was alien. The rush he still had from the sense of being in control flowed through him, in his blood; he felt high. He made his way back to Alice and handed her a glass of cold water. She still sat on the floor, and when she saw his face, she smiled.

"You okay?" he asked, sitting down on the chair beside her.

She nodded. "Just have a stinging arse and, unlike you, I didn't get an orgasm, just bruised hip bones from your table." She drank some of the water, put the glass down and gazed into his eyes. "Can I put my head on your lap for a while, please?"

Jonah sat back so she could use his legs as a cushion, and patted his knee. "Thank you, Alice." He stroked her hair.

The rush was slowly wearing off and he could see Alice felt uncomfortable and didn't look entirely happy. He lifted her by the shoulders.

"Crawl onto my lap and tell me what's on your mind, you look as though you need a hug."

As he held her, she cried softly in his arms. Through her sniffles she snuggled against his chest. "Sorry, I love being a submissive and I had a lot of fun tonight, and I know you don't like me in a romantic way, which is fine. I guess I just need a bit of release after that, too. You are very intuitive and have great ideas, and I know I am here for your pleasure, as I said earlier. But may I make a request, Jonah, sir?"

"Of course you may." He stopped stroking her hair as she looked up at him, teary eyed and cute.

She frowned. "May I please have an orgasm?" She batted her eyelashes at him before hastily adding, "Any way it pleases you, of course."

Jonah thought for a moment and then stood with her still in his arms. She really weighed nothing. "Let's go have a bath and I'll think about it."

He took her to the bathroom in the Master's suite, and left her standing in the corner while he opened the faucets on the sunken tub. "Would you like bubbles?" He looked at her as she tried to cover her nudity with her hands.

All the bravado and cheekiness had gone from her. "Yes please," she murmured.

Steam filled the room and the water thundered into the large tub into which Jonah poured scented bubble-bath. He swiftly stripped and climbed in before beckoning for Alice to join him.

"Come sit in front of me, sit with your back to my chest."

When Alice leaned tentatively against him he pulled her close. She had loosely knotted her hair on top of her head to keep it dry, and he smelled her shampoo, peaches and citrus in his nose.

With her body against his, Jonah stroked her soft, flat stomach and ran his hand gently over her lower body, testing her reaction to the sensation. She initially stiffened in his arms, but then relaxed her head back onto his shoulder.

"So, you think you deserve an orgasm?" he asked, biting her earlobe.

Alice shook her head. "I don't think I deserve one, but if sir would be kind to me I would be very grateful."

Jonah slipped his fingers between her thighs and parted the plump lips of her sex. He stroked them and listened to her soft little mewls as he increased the pressure.

She moved slowly against his hand, mumbling, "That feels so good."

Her legs parted to give him easier access, and using his index and middle fingers, Jonah squeezed her clit while sliding his fingers vertically alongside the little nub of flesh, which hardened as he handled it.

Alice ground herself on his hand, moaning louder. "Please, please, sir, don't stop."

At this Jonah bit the side of her neck and increased the speed of his hand, his fingers sliding into her on every downward stroke. She gripped the sides of the bath, and with her head on his shoulder she arched her back and let out a cry. Jonah felt her sex tighten and it seemed as though she clenched every muscle in her body as her orgasm washed over her.

Alice sighed and settled back. "Thank you. That felt incredible."

Jonah soaped a sponge and washed her front, sat her up and repeated the procedure with her back, making her stand to wash her arse and legs. "I am really glad you enjoyed yourself. I had a wonderful time. Let's get out and dry off so I can rub some cream on your bruises."

Before bed Jonah massaged a soothing lotion into Alice's hips, where they had bruised against the table, and her arse, where deep red brush marks lay evenly spread. He didn't realise he had hit her so hard.

"These marks look terrible, Alice, are you okay?" he asked, concern in his voice.

She turned her head toward him from where she lay on her stomach. "I am just fine thanks, I just have very pale skin and it marks easily, they will be gone in a day or two." She lay back down, then changed her mind. "You know, you should learn to look at marks on a submissive in a new way. It's a territorial marking, and actually, I think you'll like doing this with someone who belongs to you one day…" Her voice trailed off and Jonah put the cream aside.

"Maybe you are right, I am learning from everyone I meet, and I'm grateful." He raised the blankets so she could crawl into the bed, joined her, and turned off the light beside his bed.

As he drifted slowly off to sleep, Alice crawled into his arms and Jonah whispered, "Alice, don't fall in love with me."

Chapter 7

Anya stood at her office window, staring out at the weather, a gloomy and cold Monday. The gloom always depressed her, but she did love the sound of rain on her roof. It was a calming background noise. She took a deep breath as she heard sounds in the entrance waiting area, and tried to mentally brace herself for the next patient.

There was a soft knock at the door before the girl pushed it slowly open.

"Miss Bakos?" Anya said, stepping forward.

A bedraggled and shivering girl moved into the light of her office and nodded. She wiped her long, dyed-black hair across her forehead and tucked it behind her ear.

"Please call me Carmen."

By the end of the hour-long session with Carmen Bakos, Anya felt drained and emotional. The girl's history so closely mirrored her own it had left her feeling as though she were staring at a younger version of herself.

She needed to spend a few more hours doing paperwork at the office before heading home to Alex; she wanted to cook him a special dinner as she was feeling a bit distanced from him. Trying to focus was difficult, because her body still held the bruises of Jonah's flogging lesson, and when she closed her eyes she could imagine his hands, palms flat, running over her skin. His intoxicating smell still lingered in her memory, as did the feel of how hard he was against her that night.

She knew she and Alex needed alone time as a couple but would not get that with business, the club, and trying to run personal social lives. It was a sad reality that the club, The Realm, pretty much ruled their lives. Unease stirred in her, and she worried, because not once in her life had she thought negatively about either Alex or The Realm.

"Why is this happening to me?" she asked the universe, as she collapsed with her head on her arms.

Why was Jonah being thrown into her life? Why did she want him so badly? What was wrong? All she wanted was her inner peace back, to be content with her life, as she had been before Jonah walked into it.

***

Alex stirred as the front door opened and Anya struggled in, laden with groceries and a few bottles of wine. He watched as she placed everything on the floor, kicked off her high heels and locked the door behind her before she made her way to the kitchen. The sound of goods being stowed away was loud in the large space, and when Anya appeared in the doorway he stood.

"Hey, long day?" he asked, when he saw her face. The exhaustion was plain to see. He pulled her into a hug after she nodded. "Talk about it?"

She shook her head. "Maybe later. I am going to make you a delicious dinner and then maybe we can do something…" Her cheeks infused with colour and Alex chuckled.

"Let's see how you feel after dinner, okay? You look fit to collapse unconscious, baby."

He walked with her to the bedroom and undressed her, joined her in the shower and washed her tenderly as she groaned under his hands massaging her neck.

"Oh my goodness, that feels heavenly."

He rubbed her down with the scented body wash, using only his hands, no sponges or loofahs. When they stepped out from under the steaming jets Alex wrapped Anya in a thick fluffy towel.

"So, what is my beautiful little slave going to cook for us?" he asked, while he rubbed her dry.

She sighed. "I was craving bolognaise. We haven't had a nice dinner, just the two of us, for a while."

"Sounds delicious. I will go and switch on some music while you brush your hair into a ponytail or bun and put some socks on. Stay naked and bring me your collar when you come to the kitchen."

He left her, and in the living room, switched on the audio system. Billy Joel played throughout the house when Anya approached him holding out her collar. He fastened it around her neck while she bent her head forward.

He kissed her nose when she straightened. "There, not naked anymore."

While Anya prepared their dinner Alex poured a glass of wine for each of them. "What was so taxing about your day, pet?"

He sat down on the opposite side of the kitchen's long counter and sipped at his wine.

Anya spoke while she chopped tomatoes. "I saw an eighteen year old patient who reminded me so much of myself at that age. It was like looking in a mirror. I guess it was just draining." She glanced up at him. "What did you get up to today? Sir." She added the address almost as an afterthought, realising she was slipping and not behaving as he would expect her to.

"Well, I had a long conversation with Bartholomew about Jonah. He thinks it's a good idea to set him up with Alice. Apparently the two of them had quite a night on Friday, and Bartholomew said Alice's feedback was positive. If I didn't misunderstand him, he said she threw around terms like 'natural Dominant, slightly sadistic, very good with women's bodies' etc." He watched as Anya's hand trembled, and saw her facial muscles tighten.

She spoke while she chopped, getting more vicious as the minutes passed. "Is it really a good idea to throw someone who is still so newly out of a relationship, and inexperienced, into a Dominant/submissive dynamic?"

Her jaw was tightly set, and Alex felt the jealousy radiate off her. The dread that something bad was coming started taking a hold of him that night, and would only grow in the following months.

"Personally, Anya, I think they will be fine, it will only do him good, and they will both have fun. We know Bartholomew hardly ever gets his set-ups wrong, look at Blaine and Persephone, they will be having a collaring ceremony soon. You seem upset by the idea, though." He reached for her hand across the counter.

She looked into his eyes, confusion and unhappiness pooling in her own. "I think it's just my tiredness catching up with me. I don't know, maybe I'm hormonal, sorry."

They spoke briefly about business at The Realm, and he saw a deep weariness in her; she really was struggling tonight. Anya gazed up at him. "Do you think we will ever have a time in our life where the club doesn't have priority? I am so tired of the constant standing on ceremony, running around and rules. So many rules and people, always new initiates, old Masters… Don't you get tired of it?" She looked ashamed of the words she had just uttered and clamped her hands over her mouth. "Oh my, I am sorry sir, I know I am meant to love everything about us and our lives and our dynamic, it's just…"

Alex stroked her hair. "It's okay, I can see it's just a tough day."

He didn't mention it again, and they ate their meal in silent company while Billy Joel crooned in the background. Anya fell asleep at his feet soon after, and he carried her to bed, cradled in his arms.

When he crawled under the blankets behind her she sleepily moved against him. "I am sorry. I love you, sir, so very much."

Nothing separated their bodies, and he slid effortlessly into her while he held her folded tightly in his arms. His mouth next to her ear as he moved, Alex whispered the only words which came to mind. "Stay with me, little one, I see you slipping away. It scares me, and I don't like it…"

***

Two weeks had passed and Jonah began to realise something was up when he was faced with a smiling Alice everywhere he turned. He didn't invite her to dinner when he had his parents over to see the house, now that his furniture had arrived and the décor was finally complete.

Jonah's mother walked through the kitchen, stroking the smooth marble. "Jonah, my boy, I am so proud of you, you have a lovely home here and you have made it so nice and comfortable."

She smiled when he picked up the bottle of wine to pour a glass for each of them.

"Thanks, Mom. I am enjoying it, although it feels quite big at times." He handed her a glass, and when she took it from him he noticed there were fine lines around her mouth, and her hands didn't look as young as they used to.

With a sigh she walked out of the kitchen to find his dad in the living room, speaking as she moved. "Well, at least you won't have to move again when you get married and have little ones…"

Jonah smiled as he checked on the roast in the oven and then followed her. She was eternally optimistic that he'd find a wife and have a flock of children. His mom and dad sat together on the sofa holding hands, and when Jonah stopped in the doorway, he was struck by how much he looked forward to having that comfortable kind of love.

Jonah sat down, and they made small talk about work and pets. His parents had three dogs at home, which had been family pets during Jonah's teenage years. He gave them a brief tour of the house after dinner, bypassing the basement, and felt thoroughly glad to have seen them by the time he showed them to their car at the end of the evening.

He loved them and enjoyed their company; he would always be grateful for the wonderful childhood they'd given him. In his reading and research, Jonah had seen so many individuals who thought BDSM was full of broken and damaged people, an image the media had a hell of a good time portraying. This had made him doubt his willingness to enter a world of people who thought only men and women who'd been abused or hurt did these things. Alex seemed perfectly healthy to Jonah, though, as did Blaine and Persephone, and he hoped they could educate their peers about the joys of alternative sex, and kill the image that was so widely known. Through meeting new people he was happy to be open with, Jonah knew he would do his bit.

He locked the front door when his parents drove off, and settled down in front of his laptop in the downstairs office to do some online shopping. He wanted a butt plug and a gag, to add to his play with Alice. If they were going to be thrown together by everyone around them, he may as well learn which things he enjoyed and how to do them properly. He ended up buying a set of steel plugs. They were beautiful and could be easily sterilised. As for gags, he liked four different ones, so got a silicone ball, a rubber bit gag, a steel spider gag and a harder, plastic ball gag. He shivered in anticipation of putting those to use.

Jonah slowly strolled down to his dungeon through the monstrous empty house. He was scared, deep within his heart, of hurting Alice, but each time he saw her he liked her a little more, and against his better wishes he was getting to know her. They had fun, and the glances he caught at the last gathering when she thought he was not watching were amusing. He had found out she leaned toward monogamy too, the way he did, and he sensed she would do anything to kneel in front of him.

He stopped in the doorway to the play space and pulled the cord to turn on the light, then turned the dial to dim them. He had the polar opposite décor to Alex's dungeon. The walls were dark and the floor consisted of the same fitted hard rubber tiles, which in practicality made everything easy to clean. He had left the furniture as it was, because everything clearly had its place. The previous owners had enough experience to know how to lay it out. The armchair still stood in the corner. Jonah had placed a chest next to it, to hold the rope he had, and would purchase more soon.

All the toys he had been gifted hung on hooks against one wall, the most intimidating being a cane, narrow, shiny and scary. Though it was still lacking, he knew his collection would grow as his skills did.

He'd received an email from Alex earlier in the day enquiring about how things were going with Alice. Alex had kindly attached a document written to educate people new to BDSM about limits, both hard and soft, and how to deal with each. Jonah had not replied. He was seeing Alex for a beer after work on Monday. Alex had mentioned something about classes at The Realm, and Jonah was curious.

The limits thing was a conversation Jonah had still not had with Alice, as nothing they had done was to his mind risky enough to violate the consent she had already given him. Staring around at his dungeon, he had a thought. Jonah wanted to host the formal dinner in roughly a month's time, and he wondered if he could allow play after dinner. It would make his house feel inhabited, and would be a lovely way to end an evening, which would no doubt be filled with sexual tension and provide an intense build-up.

The thought stayed with him as he wandered to his bedroom and undressed. He brushed his teeth, mentally listing who he would invite, what he would serve and many other details.

Before Jonah dozed off, his thoughts fell on the office, and work the following week, and the inappropriate innuendos from Stavros that made him edgy. He had no idea what the man was up to, or what Stavros knew about him, but he put it aside as petty jealousy. Jonah now owned a bigger house, and to the public eye had a beautiful woman on his arm, and was content, while Stavros constantly complained about his wife, his mortgage and life in general.

Jonah put the man from his mind, took a few deep breaths and fell asleep.

***

They sat at The Refinery with a tall glass of beer and enjoyed the relaxed atmosphere on Monday evening, with the rest of the local crowd. Alex had pointed this place out as a good after work venue to Jonah when he asked him to drinks a week earlier.

Jonah turned to face him. "I want to host a high protocol type dinner, and I need your advice on who to invite. I have a basic idea of what to do, God bless the internet, so now I just need people."

Alex bobbed his head and took a deep drink of his beer. "How many people are you thinking of inviting? And where are you hosting it? Home?" He had a curious expression on his face.

Jonah started explaining his idea. "I have space for eight couples in my home, Dominants on the chairs and submissives on the floor. I want to do it at my house because I have so much space. I also haven't really had a house warming party. I thought we could have a bit of a play party after? I can accommodate five couples sleeping over." He picked up his burger and took a big bite, chewing thoughtfully while Alex did the same.

"Well, I can suggest a few guests, and Anya can instruct the submissives on how to behave on the night.

You have a lot to do, planning the menu, invitations, the list goes on. The devil is in the details." Alex put his food down and wiped his fingers. "I would love to come, and I'll take the night off from club duties when you decide on a date. Oh, as for guest suggestions, I'll email you a list a bit later."

Jonah sat listening while Alex continued making suggestions. After they finished their food and beers and stood to leave, Jonah thanked him.

"I'll be in touch." Alex gave him a hug, and Jonah spent the drive home thinking about how natural it had felt. There was no awkwardness in the physical closeness with the first man he had ever been intimate with. He kept waiting for that horrible moment when he wouldn't be able to deal with what had happened, but it never came.

When he got home Jonah walked straight to his office and picked up the stack of snow white cards he had bought and sat down behind his computer. He swiped the mouse pad to wake up the screen and spent his evening choosing designs. When the list of guest names came through from Alex, he scanned them, noticing three very familiar names: Bryce, Michael and Damian. They were three of the initiates from the night he had joined The Realm. He wondered what had happened to the fourth. He couldn't remember his name. It only came to him much later. Anderson.

Jonah printed the cards and slipped them into their matching envelopes, placing them in a neat little pile on the corner of his desk to send off the next morning. Alex had kindly included addresses in his email, and with their office courier they would be delivered on the same day.

When Jonah replied to the email he suggested a date two weeks from now, for Anya to bring the other submissives to his house and do what she needed to regarding training. The logistics of hosting the event were staggering to him as a single man, and he made a list of tasks for Alice to assist him with, and things he still needed to buy, such as extra linen to prepare the rooms. To date, he hadn't really gotten to each bedroom.

***

Plans fell together smoothly and Anya arrived at Jonah's house early on a Sunday afternoon with a large bag in her arms, looking completely at ease. After a very casual greeting and awkward hug she followed him through the dining room into the kitchen.

"They are special occasion outfits for the attending submissives," she explained, when Jonah frowned at the bag. He faked knowing what she was talking about and Anya giggled.

"I thought you'd want a unique look for the evening, so I got these put together, so the submissives would look similar, yet unique, for your event." Anya stopped in the middle of his kitchen and put her hands on her hips. "Right, before everyone gets here, could you show me around? And have you decided on a menu? Who is preparing the food?" She rapid-fired the questions at him.

Jonah held up a hand. "Woah, firstly, I have a menu idea of a starter soup, roast mains and chocolate mousse dessert. Alice makes lovely mousse. I would like the submissives to prepare the food here, before they serve it to their Dominants at the table."

Jonah failed to notice how Anya bristled at the compliment to Alice.

He showed her where everything was in the kitchen, not sure how she'd remember it all, and then took her through to the dining room. Again, he pointed out linen, crockery and cutlery, watching how closely she paid attention. The few glances they cast each other were loaded with tension and Anya seemed to avoid his gaze as much as possible. Jonah watched her as she squatted down to check the items in the cabinets and enjoyed the sight of her brushing her hair from her face. He had never stopped being in absolute awe of her natural beauty. She always seemed so effortlessly elegant, regardless of how she was dressed.

He left her in the dining room to occupy himself in his office, and heard the sound of the others arriving a short while later. At one point Jonah stood in the doorway of the kitchen, observing. Anya looked as cool and comfortable being in charge as she always did serving Alex. She stood with the submissives, all female except for one particularly attractive man with dark olive skin and hair as black as coal. Jonah knew from Alex's email this was Dimitri, one of Bartholomew's playthings. The cut of his body was evident through his shirt: he had very fine musculature, and what Jonah was sure was a low body fat percentage.

They weren't busy for long when Anya called him. "Mr. MacPherson, have you any orders or requests for the group?"

Jonah thought for a moment. "No, on the day I will need assistance readying the rooms and house, but nothing ahead of time. Thank you Anya."

Anya handed each a list of items to bring, and when they had gone she came to say goodbye to Jonah before leaving to go home herself. Again the hug they shared felt uncomfortable, and Jonah could not figure out why.

"Anya, it feels so awkward, almost uncomfortable between us, why?" he asked, stepping away from her.

Anya shrugged. "I don't know Jonah. I am having a stressful time between work, life in general and my servitude to Alex. Perhaps I am just too absorbed in worry to be good at anything right now. I'm sorry."

Jonah placed his hands on her shoulders. "Nonsense, nothing will get the better of you. You are just too good."

He pulled her into another hug, and this time she wrapped her arms tightly around him. They stood entwined like a sculpture of two lovers, and when Jonah felt her exhale slowly and soften against him, his heart started pounding. Her face lay against his neck. Her hands were on his lower back, and she stood so close he felt her thighs against his through the layers of their clothing.

This intimacy, this contact with her, was something he simultaneously craved and was terrified of. His fight or flight response kicked in and he released her, watching her stagger slightly, unbalanced for a moment. They both stood panting, and colour suffused her face. Jonah was pretty sure she could see his pulse from her vantage point, and his hands shook.

Anya blinked. "I need to go."

With that, she practically ran from the room, her ponytail swinging behind her. Jonah moved as if in a dream, walking to his front door to remotely open the gate for her as she sped down the drive. When he closed the door he turned his back to it and collapsed. He sat for a long while on the cool tile floor with his elbows resting on his bent legs, his head in his hands.

"My fucking desire for that woman will be the death of me."

He spent the rest of the afternoon behind his laptop attempting to catch up on work, but try as he might he could not focus. All Jonah smelled was Anya's perfume on his clothes, and when he closed his eyes he could still feel her soft breath on his neck. To help his craving for knowledge of her, he did what any sane person would do and Googled her name. Her surname had been on Alex's email, and Jonah found information online that left him pale and shaking in his seat.

Her past sat spread before his eyes on the computer screen, and staring at the horrific images of the car crash, Jonah wished he had never tried to satisfy his curiosity. 'Young girl orphaned in horror on the highway' the headline screamed, in bold text at the top of the screen. By the time Jonah went to bed he was no longer in any doubt about his feelings for her.

He wanted to protect her, to kiss the scars she surely carried, and to love her. He fell into his bed kissing the chance of that goodbye, though. What could he do that Alex was not doing, or had not already done? What chance did he stand? As he closed his eyes all he could see was the child beside the wreckage, and in his dreams he heard the cries, smelled the blood. He woke with a start at two thirty in the morning, and on a whim dressed in warm clothing to sit on his patio with a whiskey to calm his mind, watching the stars and drifts of cloud. He eventually went back to bed, only to be cruelly awakened by his alarm clock a few short hours later.

***

Monday found Jonah thoroughly bored at the office. He had been thinking for quite a while about changing his life and working privately, starting his own accounting business. He knew he could easily acquire the capital, and he certainly had the skills. Little did he know, destiny was about to make his life choices for him.

Alice walked toward his office wearing a white dress covered in deep red roses. It had the classic nineteen fifties style waistline and flared widely over her hips, to below her knees. She waited in his doorway drawing the eye of every man in the vicinity.

"Hey," she said, approaching him and kissing his cheek when he stood to greet her.

"Hey yourself. That's quite a dress." Jonah couldn't help but smile at the shyness pervading her demeanour. She held a box in her hands, and placed it down on his desk. "I brought you cupcakes. I baked them and thought you might need a Monday pick-up. I can't stay though." She stood blushing, and looked to him for approval.

"I really did. Thank you Alice. I'll walk you out?" Jonah placed a hand on her back and guided her toward the elevator. Inside, he dropped a quick kiss on her soft lips. "You shouldn't come here. Some of these guys are so lewd, the way they looked at you. It's like they are starving and you're a lamb chop…"

She giggled. "I guess I should feel flattered?"

Jonah smacked her arse playfully. "You should be careful."

He followed her to her car and watched her drive off, bracing himself for the comments when he got back to the office.

His instinct had been spot on. Jonah walked right into Stavros sitting in his office chair. He frowned. He wasn't particularly close friends with this man, and had a bad feeling about him on the whole. "What can I do for you Stavros?" he asked, mildly irritated at having to deal with him right now.

Stavros leered, a deeply unpleasant expression on his face. "So rich boy is fucking Barbie. That, my friend, is a nice piece of ass. Is she the one who came to 'serve' you a while ago?" he said, and reached for the cupcakes.

Jonah's temper flared. "Don't touch those." He moved the box from reach. "Listen, Stavros, I am not sure what I ever did to you, but I would very much appreciate it if you didn't make such inappropriate comments about a female acquaintance of mine. Please get out of my chair. I have a lot of work to do. Friends don't talk to friends like that, by the way."

Stavros moved from Jonah's chair, and as he got to the door he stopped. "What you can do for me is give me your 'female acquaintance's' number." He winked. "I can show her a good time with a real man. She can serve me any day."

Jonah saw red, and before he had clearly thought through his actions, Stavros was on the floor and he stood over the man, gripping his shirt collar tightly, his fist poised to strike.

"I have tried ignoring your rude comments and your petty jealousy, and the theft of a card personally addressed to me, but today you crossed a line. Stay away from me." Jonah dropped the man's head to the ground and straightened himself, walking away and going straight to his boss's office.

Jonah briefly explained the incident and stood waiting for a response while his boss stared in disbelief at him.

"Jonah, why don't you go home for the day and let the idiot calm himself and cool off? I don't need another, possibly worse, situation. You realise you face a disciplinary hearing if he lodges a complaint?"

It was an unbelievable notion. "I am not the one who started this, Mr. Jones, surely you understand that?" He ran a hand through his hair.

His boss looked tired as he replied. "I know, and the sad thing is, I can't do anything about it. The company is partially owned by that man's family. Just go home, I'll handle it."

Jonah had not known about the involvement of Stavros's family in the firm, and paled when he heard that. As he stood in the doorway facing Miles Jones, Jonah took a deep breath. "Mr. Jones, I actually know exactly what I want to do. Please accept herewith my resignation. I'll email the letter to you from home."

Miles coughed and stood. "Now Jonah, don't let one little setback make you leave a secure job..."

With a smile Jonah shook his head. "It's not one setback, Miles. I have actually been thinking about it for a while now."

With a resigned shrug Miles sat. "Well, think about it before you send me anything, okay? I'll pretend this conversation didn't happen until then. You are a good worker and it would be sad to lose you."

Jonah walked past everyone, ignoring the glares, admiring glances, and in a few cases frightened looks, as he gathered his stuff and left.

He walked out of the building, and it felt as though a huge weight dropped from his shoulders. In his car, Jonah turned up the volume on his radio to hear Sting sing quite appropriately about 'brand new days'. All felt right with the world. He knew that things were getting better, and when he walked into his house the decision he had made to resign sat firmly in his mind. It was time to move on.

He sat down behind his desk, flipped open his laptop, and spent an hour typing out a letter of resignation. He paused before clicking on the send button, not because he was unsure of his decision, but because he knew this was simply another step in the right direction. Much like joining The Realm, and buying the house, this was part of his growth.

The next few days were busy for Jonah, as he arranged the payment of his final salary and withdrew his pension fund to re-invest part of it. He kept an amount out to cover his income for three months as he started on his new venture. He could manage for the three month period until he got at least one big client to tide him over.

Between dealing with his departure from work, he did shopping and preparation for the dinner. Jonah stocked his bar, filled his fridge with the required ingredients, and hired a house keeping company for two days to clean the house from top to bottom. When they were done, the floors gleamed and his home smelled of furniture polish and detergent. It was so wonderful Jonah only used his study, and barely touched the kitchen and his bedroom out of necessity, wanting to preserve the cleanness.

All he needed was a good suit, so he spent a morning with a well-known tailor, knowing the clothing would be an investment, perfect for any functions at The Realm or out on the town.

By the time the date of the dinner arrived, everything was perfect.

Chapter 8

Jonah sat in the living room, completely relaxed and at-ease with a glass of scotch in his hand. He could hear the muted sound of women talking in the kitchen, along with the clinking of china in the dining room.

Every serving submissive had been instructed to arrive three hours prior to their Master, and in one case, Mistress. They were now cooking and setting the table, placing a tray of welcome drinks in the foyer, and making sure all would be in order.

Jonah looked forward to meeting the people Alex had advised him to invite: eight couples, out of whom he was acquainted with only six individuals. The others were a high ranking Mistress within The Realm, her submissive, and three of the initiates from his group, the ones who had settled with submissives of their own after joining. He had been briefly introduced to them on the night, but hadn't seen them since.

He looked at his watch, stood and went to find Alice; he wanted her dressed and ready to hand out welcome drinks when the guests arrived. She stood at the kitchen counter scooping chocolate mousse into dessert glasses to place in the refrigerator, but turned to face him the moment he appeared in the door.

"I want you to go and get dressed, Alice. As I told you, you will be welcoming our guests. I want you to look perfect."

Jonah patted her rump as she walked past, inducing a playful giggle. He caught the wistful glance from Anya. She was checking on the individual beef wellingtons from the oven.

She smiled. "You two seem happy."

There was so much he wanted to say to her that he rather turned away. He checked on the dining room, and saw Dimitri, the one slave accompanying Bartholomew, folding napkins and sliding them carefully into the silver rings. Every piece of wood in the room gleamed in the soft light. The table stood immaculate, and Jonah looked appreciatively at the man. He was handsome, with his dark hair and olive skin, and was dressed in a casual pair of jeans and a T-shirt.

Dimitri noticed him in the doorway. "I am all done Master Jonah, do you mind if I go to prepare myself?" He had an exotic, strange accent.

Jonah stepped aside, gesturing to the stairs. "Of course you may. You know which bathroom has been designated for the slaves to change, and shower or bath?"

He nodded at Jonah, and with his eyes down he left the dining room. Jonah was growing more comfortable with the manner in which the submissives of The Realm handled themselves toward all Dominants and Masters. He loved that there was so much respect involved. He had so far only seen love and returned respect given by the Masters. Regardless of the activities, care and emotion were always present, be it during or after play.

***

At seven p.m., the other guests started arriving. Alice stood beside the tray of champagne flutes, curtsying deeply to each arriving guest before she handed them a glass and led them through to Jonah in the living room.

Jonah stood to greet them, and then kept up the polite chatter until the next one joined. Each new person complimented him on Alice's appearance, behaviour and dress. It had been agreed that the slaves and submissives would wear the diaphanous garments similar to those they wore at the club. Each had been gifted with a sheer black set Anya had brought to Jonah's house when she'd initially brought the slaves. These garments were cuffed only at the wrists, so that individual collars of ownership could be worn. Jonah made a note to thank Anya for the attention to detail; it worked really well and added to the atmosphere.

Alice wore no collar, as Jonah did not own her, and they had not entered into the formal bond of Master and slave. Dimitri, instead of being dressed in the feminine item of clothing, wore black pants made of a stretchable fabric suited to kneeling, and was shirtless. His neck bore a heavy, black leather collar with a ring at the base of his throat. Below the ring, his muscles rippled smoothly from his pecs to the deep V of his abdominals, which disappeared into the black fabric.

The slaves knelt in perfect poses in a row beside the fireplace in the living room, moving to greet and join their owners as they arrived, and then sit at their feet. They did not speak to other Masters or to each other. At the start of the evening, as instructed, they would only speak to their owner if and when spoken to. Their place was to silently observe the needs of their owners, fill empty glasses, serve dinner, and clean up afterwards.

At Alex's suggestion, Anya was in charge of the rest of them, and would make sure everything ran smoothly. She would serve Alex and monitor the other slaves, using hand signals if something were being neglected. Jonah chatted briefly to Bryce, Michael and Damian, the three men whom he had met on his initiation night, and watched as they fondly stroked the heads of their respective girls.

Bartholomew seemed pleased with himself and looked like a monarch of old sitting in a luxurious armchair with his two slaves at his feet. Laila looked ethereal as always, all pale skin, pale hair and pale eyes. She was the perfect polar opposite of Dimitri, who knelt beside her.

At a signal from Anya, all the slaves stood to follow her from the room. It was time for dinner. Jonah's gaze followed Anya, her walk mesmerizing, her skin beckoning to his hands. She had barely spoken to him all afternoon, she was so occupied with preparation, but her looks said more than words ever could and Jonah sensed she was in turmoil about something.

He stood. "Would everybody please make their way to the dining room, dinner is ready," he said.

His eyes fell on Samantha, the only Mistress in the room. The woman intimidated him. She was roughly his height in a pair of black stiletto boots, ending just above her knees and leaving a thin stretch of pale skin exposed below where her tight, black leather miniskirt started. Her corset cinched everything tightly together, her breasts peeking over the top. Samantha's hair was slicked into a smooth, deep red, bobbed cut, and her makeup, deep red lips and dark eyeliner, completed the all-around terrifying guise. You did not have to look into her eyes twice to know she was Dominant; it showed in every imperious gesture and every posh accented word she spoke. Jonah cleared his throat as he sat and allowed Alice to slide his chair in for him.

"Samantha, you have a lovely accent, where are you from?" he asked politely.

She focused her dark eyes on him intently. "Thank you, Jonah, I was born in England, my parents lived just outside London. We relocated to the United States when I finished college, and have been here since. They are in New York, though, and I am here, to be closer to my Olga."

Jonah dipped his head as he picked up his glass, which was filled to the perfect level with rich red wine. He briefly glanced at the girl beside Samantha, a lovely little thing. Just like Laila she had pale hair and eyes, again, the opposite to her Mistress. *They are yin and yang*, he thought to himself, *so different and yet so similar*.

As soon as everybody was settled in their seats with appropriate drinks, the slaves appeared holding bowls of sundried tomato, basil and pecorino soup, and small rounds of toast. The starter was set down with great care before the slaves returned to the kitchen to fetch their own, settling upon their return diagonally behind their respective owners. Usually the slaves would only eat after their owners had finished their meal, but tonight Jonah wanted everyone finished more or less simultaneously, so play would not go on too late for those driving home.

The meal passed smoothly until Olga's heel caught on the carpet and she tripped, spilling a single potato off Samantha's plate onto her placemat. The Mistress leapt from her seat the moment the plate was securely set down and swung to face Olga, who had turned pale and was staring fixedly at Samantha's feet.

"I am so sorry Mistress, my shoe caught on the carpet. I didn't mean to…" Her pitiful cries were cut off by a resounding slap to her cheek, and Samantha dragging her from the room by her hair.

The others completely ignored the spectacle, and as Jonah's eyes widened, Alex patted his shoulder. "Each Dominant deals differently with mishaps, mistakes and disobedience. Don't gawk. This type of dinner calls for perfect behaviour, and that slave just embarrassed her owner."

Jonah nodded and picked at his food while Alice refilled his wine glass with trembling hands. He didn't understand how Olga tripping should embarrass Samantha…

When Olga returned she was barefoot and had tears on her cheeks.

Samantha ignored the girl as she slid smoothly into her seat. "I refuse to abide clumsiness," she muttered before resuming her meal as though nothing had happened.

The slaves cleared the table after the main course, served dessert and brought coffee, while Jonah sat thinking about his talk on rules of play for the evening. He felt completely unprepared for this, being so inexperienced amongst these people. He finished his chocolate mousse and stood, watching as Alice swept the glass smoothly from view.

Jonah cleared his throat and folded his hands in front of his body. "Well, now that we have all eaten, I would like to just run through a few basic rules and guidelines for the evening. First off, those who are sleeping over, you know where your rooms are and your respective slaves have placed your overnight luggage there. Those who are driving home, please be safe and don't drink excessively. As for play, there are areas which provide some privacy, and public space too, the whole house is at your disposal. The dungeon is open, and I simply ask that you respect my equipment, not use my own toys, and leave things as you find them. Have a lovely evening!"

With nods of agreement from everybody, he moved away from the table and pulled Alice aside. "I want you to keep an eye on people, and call me if you see unsafe conduct or damage being done to my property, okay?"

The girl's smile fell from her face. "So we are not going to do anything sir?"

He shook his head. "No, not until they are all in their private rooms or have left. We, as hosts, are the responsible entities."

Alice nodded and slunk off to help with the cleaning while people still mingled around the table.

***

Over the next hour Jonah wandered through the house checking in on various scenes as they unfolded, most mesmerized by Damian and Mimi in the dungeon. The Dominant had laid out a bag and towel on the medical table, having pulled it close to the chains that hung from the ceiling. Mimi was tied and gagged, her arms tightly folded behind her back in a box-tie. Her breasts stood out, exaggerated by the pressure of the rope, and Damian stood handling them tenderly.

Jonah watched as he smiled at Mimi, and fear bloomed in her eyes. She shook her head wildly from side to side, and left Jonah wondering how she could use a safe word in such a situation. It was then he noticed the bell clutched tightly in her one hand behind her back and made the connection. If she wished to safe out all she had to do was ring it.

Damian took a breast in each hand and squeezed, eliciting semi-silenced moans from the strung-up girl. She screwed her eyes shut and her brow furrowed with concentration. Damian released her and reached for more rope. He wound it in tight binds around each breast, flicking the nipples when he completed the tie. Her breasts started changing colour, taking on a reddish-purple hue, and tears flowed freely down her cheeks. Jonah felt gooseflesh move down his spine as Damian retrieved sterile needles from his bag and unwrapped them, removed the caps and placed them on the towelled surface he had readied.

Damian snapped black, nitrile gloves onto his hands and sprayed them with disinfectant, Mimi's eyes following his every movement. Stepping up to her again, he held one breast firmly, tweaked the swollen nipple, and so slowly that Jonah barely saw it all, slid the needle through it. Jonah looked from Damian's hands to Mimi's face, and saw her eyes close, her head falling back. She was breathing, but seemed lost in some other world. He left, giving them privacy, and headed to his office, where he had heard the sounds of a cane earlier on.

All he heard now was a hysterical sobbing that awakened all his protective instincts. When he peered around the door he saw Anya spread out on his desk, and Alex leaning over her with his hand tangled in her hair. Jonah stopped to watch, his gaze travelling over Anya's back to her arse, where red and livid stripes lay perfectly spaced all the way to the backs of her knees. As he closed his eyes and took a deep breath Jonah heard a mobile phone ring and saw Alex stiffen. He released Anya's hair, and while still keeping a hand on her back he fished his phone from his pocket. He listened briefly and then let loose a string of expletives fit to make a sailor blush. When he saw Jonah he beckoned him over.

"Jonah, I need to go, there's been an accident at the club. Please can you take over and look after Anya, she can't be alone after the beating she just took for me, and I wasn't done with her yet." He grabbed his jacket and gave Anya a kiss on her forehead.

"Will Alice let me out?" he asked as he pulled himself to a stop in the doorway.

Jonah nodded, too distracted by Anya's state to pay much attention. "Yes, she is around, just find her."

Jonah heard the door open and shut and breathed deeply. "Anya," He placed a hand between her shoulder blades, "Come here."

Jonah reached down and lifted her off the desk, picking her up and sitting down in the large armchair with her on his lap. He pulled a soft blanket, from the foot stool, over her, covering her nudity while he softly stroked her hair.

She calmed eventually and sat up in Jonah's lap, rubbed her eyes and looked deeply into his. "He left me? He left because of that club. I am so tired of this, it's always 'the club this, we need to go to the club, I have work'. Never ending." She unexpectedly put her arms around his neck and nuzzled close to him. Sobs wracked her small frame, and all Jonah could do was hold her.

"He left me like this, in this state. He knows how I get after heavy pain play and he still left me to go to his precious club..." Her voice trailed off as she began kissing the sides of his neck.

Jonah closed his eyes. "Anya, do you think it's a good idea for you to be doing that?"

He cleared his throat and held her away from his body. Her eyes were mildly glazed over when he held her face in his hands, and something he had read came back to him, about the idea of subspace...

Her voice was husky when she spoke. "Jonah, I don't care about should or shouldn't or right or wrong, for once I want to do exactly what I want to do, no permission, no orders."

Jonah completely lost his train of thought as she lowered her face to his.

***

The world disappeared when Anya's lips met Jonah's. She had never experienced the sensation before, and all her heartache over Alex leaving vanished. The pain from the stripes on her arse became unimportant. All that mattered was them, that the contact not be broken, that she have him. She adjusted her position and sat straddling Jonah's lap.

They were so drowned in each other, neither of them saw Alice's face as she stuck her head around the door to check if everything was okay, nor did Alice stick around to see what happened a few short minutes later.

Jonah focused and pushed Anya back, shaking his head. "This is not how I want this to happen, Anya. Not with you raw because Alex left you, or with his marks all over your body." Jonah rubbed his eyes.

Anya stared at him, shock on her beautiful tear streaked face. "How you want what to happen?" she asked, her voice scared and confused.

He allowed his vulnerability to show. "You and me, this, kissing you, feeling you naked in my arms. My feelings where you are concerned are too strong to allow having you to be merely the consequence of someone else's actions."

Anya stood on shaky legs. "You have feelings for me? Since when, Jonah? You and Alice are together." She walked small circles around the room. "This was just going to be a…" She threw up her arms in frustration. "I don't know. I am so confused, all I wanted was some physical release."

Jonah stood and pulled her into an embrace. "I have had feelings for you I can't explain since I brushed past you in that club the first night we met. I have been scared of being around you since I found out you belong to Alex, because I never want to cause trouble, quite frankly, nor do I want to get hurt. You are my Kryptonite in this whole kink world I have been pulled into, head over heels. I can do everything without emotion, except you. I know Alex keeps talking about your open relationship, but that's not me, I just can't." He rubbed her back as he held her and felt her shake gently as she cried.

"Jonah, please can you walk me to my room? I think I need to go to bed."

Anya never told him how she felt about him as he took her to the bedroom she was supposed to share with Alex for the night. She kissed his cheek when she closed the door before collapsing into the fluffy down duvet in a fresh fit of sobs. She never felt the cane cuts on her arse burst and did not notice the blood sticking to the sheets as she pulled them over herself in the dark.

It felt like hours had passed when Jonah finally went looking for Alice. He found her in the living room curled up on the couch, dressed in a soft tracksuit, not asleep but quiet. She looked up at him and he saw the fresh hurt there.

"Why are you here all alone Alice?" Jonah sat down beside her.

She shrugged. "They have gone, or gone to bed. Everyone. I went to find you so that we could maybe play, but I saw you with Anya…"

He let out a heavy sigh. "Yes, Alex had to leave, there was an emergency at the club and he asked me to look after her. She had been caned heavily."

Alice sat up, pulling a throw around her shoulders. "I know." She gazed intently into his eyes. "Jonah, sir, I remember you warning me not to fall in love with you the first time I spent the night with you. Why is that? Don't people just do this and see what happens? Why don't you think you can love me? I have tried so hard to please you."

Jonah tried to fathom what she wanted to know, exactly, and answered with care. "I have recently come out of a long relationship, and I am not ready to be in another. I don't want to hurt anyone, Alice, that's why I warned you. I think my own 'happy ever after' is a while away."

She nodded. "I get it. I saw you kiss Anya, by the way. That was not a kiss between strangers. I think you love her."

With that Alice stood. "Excuse the lack of subservience in my demeanour, but I wish to kneel to a man who respects me and loves me, and I thought I could make you love me, only me, but I see now I was wrong. I am going to get my stuff and head home, I haven't had anything to drink so I'll be fine."

Before she left the room, and Jonah, who was deeply confused, she turned back.

"I don't think your 'happy ever after' is as far away as you think. She loves you too, you know, it's obvious." Alice flung her hair over her shoulder and left.

"I'm sorry, Alice. I didn't mean for this to happen."

Jonah knew she would be hurting for a while.

He went to check briefly on Anya before going to bed and saw her in the moonlight, curled in the centre of the bed with the covers pulled over her. He closed her door silently and walked into his own bathroom, climbed into a steaming shower and then fell, exhausted, into his bed.

The next morning Jonah made sure everyone was safely on their way, watching them climb into their cars and drive off. Alex arrived before Anya was up and only briefly greeted Jonah before going to her.

He heard her angry screaming, and the fight that ensued, all the way down in the kitchen. When they came down the stairs, Anya behind Alex, both were subdued and she refused to make eye contact even when she mumbled, "I am sorry, there's blood on the bedding from my cuts."

They said goodbye and left without Jonah getting to discuss the kiss which had taken place the previous night.

He had wanted to do so over coffee, in a private space, no Alex, no intrusion, and no subspace or confusion.

He was alone at last and poured a mug of strong coffee from the jug, before he walked out onto his back patio muttering to himself. "What a fucking disaster."

So much for the lovely dinner he had envisioned, he thought, or the fun evening. All it had been was emotional and tiring. He finished his coffee and spent the day cleaning and tidying.

Jonah hadn't arranged cleaners again, he was concerned about inappropriate items left behind and wanted to do the sweep of the house himself. After the third bed he stripped, he realised he definitely wanted someone else to do this. With a few choice expletives he continued the arduous task, all the while wondering if Anya and Alex would be okay.

***

It took a while for Jonah to get a reply from Alex as to having an afternoon beer. He wanted to talk about everything that had happened on the night of the dinner. He hadn't heard from Anya, either, and the total lack of communication worried him. He now sat in the BistroRx with a tall glass in front of him while he waited for Alex.

When the other man walked through the door Jonah saw the exhaustion in his eyes and his movements. He stood to greet him and they both sat.

"Hey, sorry to say this, but you look terrible, Alex, what's up?" Jonah asked as he beckoned a waiter over.

"Just having some trouble with the club and with Anya. I am a bit tired." Alex ordered a beer and sat back. "Enough of my shit. What's new on your front? Catch me up."

Jonah told him about the end of the evening that he had missed, about breaking up with Alice, and about the work drama which had led to his resignation. Jonah still had no regrets about his decision, and spent a good number of hours each day sending proposals to prospective clients and re-organising his office to suit full-time work.

Alex straightened in his seat when Jonah spoke of the fact that he would now be working for himself, and stopped his flood of words with a raised hand. "Wait, what? You quit your job, am I getting this straight?"

Jonah nodded and Alex started laughing.

"This is so awesome!" He held up a hand. "I don't mean awesome that you quit your job under crap circumstances, but I have had issues with the accountant for the club, he is relocating to New York. If you are keen on taking over, the work is yours, and it pays well. We might be closed for a while until things settle after Friday night, but as soon as we are sorted out the job is yours, if you want it."

It took a while for them to discuss the details, and Jonah accepted without hesitating. The pay Alex offered was indeed very good. Before they left the bar Alex placed a hand on Jonah's shoulder.

"I understand how confusing things are with Anya. Don't worry about the awkwardness. I think she is dealing with a few inner questions about what she wants from life. She hasn't been herself lately. She will figure it out, as she always does, and all will be well again." He walked Jonah to his car, his own motorbike parked nearby. "As for Alice, it's a pity that didn't work out. She is a lovely girl."

Jonah shrugged. "She could have been Miss USA and I still wouldn't have been able to develop an emotional attachment to her. I don't know why these things happen, but she just wasn't right for me."

He got into his car. Alex had started walking away, but turned back.

"That sucks, I almost forgot, we are doing a bit of a meditation, 'finding your inner voice' type thing on Tuesday evening at The Realm, you should come, seven p.m. Calm space after the accident."

Jonah frowned. "What happened, Alex? It sounds serious, if you might have to close."

Alex shrugged. "It's nothing, I'll be in touch."

With that he turned away, leaving Jonah puzzled and curious. Alex slipped his helmet on, and with a roar of the bike's engine, sped off. Jonah never saw the worry crease his brow, the knowledge clear that the only woman Jonah wanted a tie to was his Anya, and he knew Jonah was not open to polyamory...

Alex was breaking a little each day, and he couldn't tell a soul.

Plus, he now had to deal with an extra stress: his business may not survive.

Chapter 9

The message to go to Alex's home for the meditation evening, as opposed to the club, came late on Monday afternoon. Jonah again found himself worried about what was happening.

Jonah arrived at Alex's place, entering through the lower parking lot to a large room which was dimly lit. Candles filled every alcove and surface and soft classical music played throughout. Jonah loved that the music at any gatherings of members of The Realm was always mood-enhancing, not too loud to hold a conversation, and activity appropriate. He stopped into the entrance and saw Alex stand to come and greet him.

Cushions and throw blankets covered the floor, and in the circle sat Bartholomew, raised on a dais of bigger pillows, calmly watching the others. Jonah saw Blaine and Persephone, all the other initiates of his group, and several people he did not recognise.

Alex took him by the arm. "Come find a spot, you can sit with Anya and I, if you wish. I am so sorry for the change, I just didn't want to cancel this."

He hushed Jonah when he tried to ask questions.

"We will all take some time to quiet our minds, just sit and breathe deeply and slowly, and I'll answer your questions when I can, okay?" Alex whispered this when Jonah frowned, and then released his arm. "When everybody is here, Bartholomew will do a guided meditation."

With a final nod Jonah sat down beside Anya, arranging his cloak comfortably. She smiled as Jonah joined them and then turned her face back to Bartholomew. They sat in silence. All Jonah could hear was the soft inhales and exhales as he joined them in trying to clear his mind. There were new lines on Alex's face which Jonah could not help but notice.

Jonah looked around at all the heads in front of him and saw Alice beside Bartholomew. Obviously she had decided to join his little family of slaves. Laila and Dimitri sat on either side of her, their fingers intertwined. The slaves were in normal clothing this evening, soft looking cotton t-shirts and track pants. The women wore their hair in different styles, having clearly come from normal jobs, not dressed specially for an 'occasion' and some wore makeup. There was no need for ceremony here. The only thing that stood out, letting on this was a 'Realm' activity, was the men in their cloaks.

Twenty minutes passed and three or more people arrived, then Jonah heard the doors lock and silence descended over everybody present. Bartholomew stood and walked among them; he was barefooted and emanated a calm authority. As Jonah watched, he stopped beside each individual and laid a hand on their head. When he spoke his voice entranced Jonah.

"Good evening all. This is the first of the meditations the new initiates are attending, and I want to explain what our goal is here. We will clear our minds of the day's chaos and thoughts of work and family. Breathe deeply and be in the moment. Being calm allows us to hear our inner voices and listen to what our hearts need. I know it sounds 'cheesy' to our younger members perhaps, but try." Bartholomew reached Jonah, and as he touched his hair, Jonah's mind cleared of all the worry: Alice, Anya, work, the future, it all disappeared.

"Each of you has a desire, be it monetary or romance related, physical goals or more spiritual. We all dream of something specific to happen in our lives. I want you to let that blank space that's now in your mind, which this calm has brought you, be filled with which you most desire."

Bartholomew continued his circuit of the people, and finally sat down again, beckoning his slaves closer and touching their heads tenderly.

With a deep breath Jonah focused on what he most wanted, and his mind was filled with Anya. He saw a future with her so clearly it hurt. He saw their family, their wedding, the love and pain that would lead to those things. He saw all of this before he realised what he had just shown Bartholomew, who had surely read his mind along with every other person's here.

When Jonah opened his eyes Bartholomew was staring straight at him and shaking his head. Jonah closed his eyes and tried again, to see something different, but it was to no avail, he wanted only Anya. He had everything else he could desire. It was just her presence in his life in this context which eluded him still.

They sat like that for an hour, during which Jonah felt the confusion emanate from Anya beside him, and the worry from Alex. He was amazed that so much sensation could be rippling through him all at once. It was the strangest experience he had ever had.

At the end of the hour, he stood, and wracked with confusion and worry for what the future of his desires held, he left without saying goodbye to anyone, ashamed of what he had exposed.

***

Alex walked straight to Bartholomew after the session, having felt his call, and stopped about a metre away while he spoke with Alice. When Bartholomew called Alex closer, he had a concerned expression on his face.

"Do you know how badly Jonah MacPherson desires your slave?" he asked, not wasting time with small talk.

Alex shook his head. "I know there is chemistry between them, but I didn't see anything to worry about."

"Open your eyes, Alex. That man sees his entire future, a monogamous one, with Anya. I saw it in his thoughts. He loves her."

Alex flinched at his words. "And does Anya feel the same?" His voice sounded dead to himself.

Bartholomew nodded. "She does have extremely strong feelings for him, but she doesn't know the extent of them as yet. I sense she is in denial. She is deeply unhappy in her relationship with you, though, and feels that this business and The Realm take precedence over her. She knows she has the responsibility of being grateful to you because of her past, but she wonders if perhaps her debt is paid. I don't think you can fix what has broken in her, not this time, my friend…" Bartholomew placed a hand on his shoulder. "Just prepare yourself, Alex. She may be entering a phase of difficult decisions in her life, and you might lose her."

Alex felt as though he limped away from the conversation when he walked back to Anya. He pulled her into an embrace and stood holding her. When she raised a questioning eyebrow at him, Alex kissed her.

"You know how much you mean to me, don't you?"

She nodded. "I do, I am sorry I've been distant and obstinate, I just have a lot on my mind."

He pulled her close again. "Whatever it is, we will work it out, okay? One way or another."

Part Three

Chapter 10

The weeks following the meditation session were tumultuous for Anya and Alex. Between her building resentment of the twenty-four seven power exchange between them, and Alex's growing fear of the distance in her eyes, they were on a downhill path toward a crash.

The club issues had been resolved, with only a minor loss of a few days; not as serious as Alex had been worried about. Keeping the accident out of the news and avoiding an enormous scandal, as well as dealing with Anya's issues, had left Alex exhausted.

***

It took Anya many hours of deep thought and careful examination of her feelings to come to the decision that would make or break her life. She hid in her office, masking her isolation with the guise of work. Fewer patients passed through her door during those weeks due to her need for space, and yet she couldn't face going home at night.

When she finally took a deep breath to plunge into either bliss or oblivion, it was with fear and trepidation that she went to her home, perhaps for the last time. She sat in her car for a long while before going inside, silently bidding everything familiar farewell.

***

Anya sat in her office waiting for Alex to come home from work; he had been at the club again. It was four in the morning and she felt raw. In front of her desk, the suitcases were neatly stacked with her collar on top of them. She still had no idea if she was doing the right thing, and she cried quietly as she thought of what she was potentially throwing away. She doubted she could be friends with Alex after all they'd shared, but her heart broke with the knowledge that she was going to hurt him deeply today, after all he had done for her.

She picked up the envelope containing the letter she'd written last night, while he was out. She walked into the main bedroom, the room they had shared for years now, and placed it on his pillow. It was long, and a more in depth explanation than she would be able to give him to his face. She knew he would read it because he was not one to react in anger. She also had a suspicion he knew this may be coming after her withdrawn nature over the past few weeks.

Anya walked back into her office and sat down. The knowledge of how strong her feelings for Jonah were had hit her the first time she had heard about him playing with Alice so long ago. It had hurt a little more every time she saw them, or heard of them, thereafter. She tried not to think about the kiss she had shared with him. It had been an experience she would never forget until the day she died.

She had slowly become lost in the misery of how badly she wanted him to be with her, and knowing she could not have both Alex and Jonah. Jonah was wholeheartedly monogamous and unwilling to change, so she had to take this step, cause and endure the pain she was about to walk into, all to risk perhaps still not having Jonah after all. How could she know, with certainty, if he felt the same? He was with Alice now, wasn't he? And what he had said that night after they'd kissed — he could be have been lying or caught up in the moment.

Anya had not seen or heard from him in a while, having immersed herself in her work during this period of inner warfare. Anya had succeeded in avoiding the club for several weeks now, using her patients as an excuse.

***

When Alex entered the room later, while looking for her, he found her collapsed with her head in her arms on her desk, fast asleep. He looked at the suitcases and the collar so neatly placed on top, and felt his heart tear apart.

He scrawled a note and left it beside her, saying, 'I'm in the living room when you are ready.' Then he left, taking the collar with him as he fell onto his sofa. His gut had told him this was coming, and he had held out on confronting Anya about her behaviour, seeing how she wrestled with the feelings she had for Jonah and her doubts about her relationship.

Alex had sensed her reluctance to be around Jonah after the first kiss they'd shared. The chemistry between them had been incredible from the first meeting, hadn't it? Alice had told him in detail, when she came crying to him about her relationship with Jonah not succeeding. Alex fondled the collar, the leather worn and soft in his hands, and remembered the day he had given it to her.

It was not his intention to show emotion today, and he wiped miserably at his eyes, sharply looking up when he heard movement in the doorway.

Anya stood there with her head hanging, hair tangled and unkempt, dressed in faded jeans and a stripy sweater. "I'm sorry."

They were the first and only words out of her mouth before she knelt down in front of him and laid her head on his legs. She held onto the knees of his pants and started crying.

Alex put a hand on her shaking head. "It's okay love. I know this hurts both of us, trust me, but you know your own heart and mind, and need to do what you feel is right."

Anya raised her face to him, her eyes molten, red rimmed and filed with tears. "I don't know what's right, but I can't keep being like this, only half present. It's not fair to either of us."

"I agree," he said, stroking her hair. "Do you have a place to stay?"

Her face was incredulous as she spoke. "I am hurting you, leaving, and instead of being mean or petty your first concern is that I have a place to stay? Oh my God! Can you not be so perfect for once?" She sobbed even harder than before.

Alex was working very hard to maintain his own composure at this point, and cleared his throat. "You don't need my anger or resentment, Anya, even if you feel you deserve that reaction. You are hurting just as badly. I will lick my wounds in private, so I am going to call you a cab and then we are going to part ways. We might not see each other for a while, but I care for you, and if you need help, you come and tell me, okay?" He lifted her face, made sure she acknowledged him, and then tenderly kissed her forehead.

"I will see you again at the club, I am sure. Be a good girl, and I wish you all the best."

Alex stood, walked into the kitchen, and called a cab. Then he went straight to his bedroom, seeing the envelope on his pillow. After stripping off, he climbed in the shower. Alex stood under the stream of scalding water for a long while, and when he came out again, Anya was gone.

***

After the end of his relationship with Anya, it was tough, but Alex knew he had to keep up the face he showed to the world, to the club. He attended events while Anya seemingly disappeared into the ether. Bartholomew had let Alex know that Anya had come to him, to explain that she needed a bit of time away to think things through, and wished him well for the future.

Alex saw her everywhere: in the shape of the bowed submissives, wrapped in his bedclothes, he smelled her perfume whenever he turned his head. Everybody thought Dominants, and men in general, to be void of emotion, but nobody saw Alex cry about the loss of her.

Nobody saw him break until several weeks after she had left, when Jonah unexpectedly entered his private chambers looking for him. It was a special night, a collaring ceremony was taking place, and Alex had gone off to seek quiet from the gushy happiness on the main floor.

"Alex?" Jonah called around the doorframe, and when he poked his head into the room, Jonah saw the saddest sight he had ever witnessed. Alex sat on the floor at the foot of his bed, clutching Anya's collar in his hands. He hastily wiped his face and made to rise when he saw Jonah, but was stopped by Jonah's hand on his shoulder.

"What is it? Are you okay?" Jonah asked, putting his arm around Alex.

With his voice gruff Alex faced him. "We broke up a while ago. I am surprised you haven't heard. She left me."

The meaning of the words didn't dawn on Jonah for several moments. "What? You guys were the perfect couple, how did this happen?" He stopped asking questions when Alex stared blankly at him.

With a big sigh Alex stood and straightened his clothing out. "Anya felt indebted to me for a long time, and she loved me very much, just as I love her still. She needed a break from the intensity of our dynamic and she felt neglected. I work too much, and pretty much every facet of my life is involved with The Realm. She couldn't deal with that anymore."

"No, I can't accept that." He folded his arms across his chest. "Have you heard from her since she left?"

"I am giving her space. I trust she would talk to me if she needed anything. Jonah, I know you love her, Bartholomew told me. If you really care for her, if you can promise me now that you will never hurt that girl, I give you my full blessing to go and tell her what you saw and felt at the meditation session. But so help me I will kill you if you treat her badly." Alex faced him squarely, and Jonah sank to his knees in front of him.

"Alex, I couldn't hurt her if I tried. I would never do that. I want her in my life. I have known this from our first accidental touch, to the one kiss we shared. She is meant for me, only her."

Alex nodded once and placed a hand on Jonah's head. "Then I formally give you my blessing to go to her. Help her, because I know she is hurting. I can feel it."

He lifted his hand and left Jonah kneeling on his floor.

***

Back at his house, Jonah sat down in his study. He chose the armchair where he had cuddled Anya, remembering the sensation of her body in his arms, and later, her lips on his. It had been a beautiful night, getting to watch Blaine put a collar of ownership around Persephone's neck in a formal ceremony. It had been the BDSM equivalent of a wedding, and every bit as beautiful, if not more so.

He picked up the cup of coffee he'd brought with him and cradled it in his hands. The clock showed it was two thirty a.m., and even though he was exhausted Jonah's mind was stuck on how he would go about finding Anya. He didn't know where she was staying, nor did he know her work address. As he thought of her work he leapt up.

"Bless the internet!" he exclaimed, walking to his desk to flop down into the chair there, splashing a stack of work with coffee in his excitement.

He found her business details with one search, and wrote down the telephone number and address on a notepad he dug out from under a pile of papers. Now all Jonah had to do was think of what he would say to her. He knew all the preparation in the world couldn't ready him for facing her, but he needed at least a basic plan.

Jonah got caught up tidying his paperwork after cleaning the coffee spill. After that he decided he was so thoroughly awake he may as well work, so he fetched a second cup of coffee and fell on the club's books with gusto. When Jonah's phone rang at seven in the morning, he was hyped up on caffeine and buzzing from lack of sleep.

"Hey," he answered, not checking who it was. The voice on the other side of the line caught him completely off guard.

"It's Anya speaking, Jonah. I was wondering if you would like to have coffee? I want to apologise for my vanishing act, and it would be nice to see a familiar face,.."

She sounded lonely and depressed, and as Jonah sat trembling, he answered. "Oh, oh wow. Yes! I need to see you."

When she didn't reply Jonah realised he had sounded a bit manic. "I am sorry I sound crazy, haven't slept at all and I think I've had eight cups of coffee since two this morning…"

Anya giggled. "That's not healthy. You should be careful, so much caffeine is bad for your heart."

The tension broken, Jonah asked Anya to dinner at his house. He only realised afterward that it was perhaps not the wisest idea to be in close proximity to a bed, or so secluded. She had just come out of a hell of a relationship and the last thing he wanted to be was her rebound guy.

"Anya," he said when they were about to hang up. "It is good to hear from you."

She ended the call.

***

Two days later, Jonah stood at his kitchen counter rubbing olive oil, rosemary, coarse salt flakes and ground black pepper into a lamb roast, just as his mom had instructed. The sun made its slow arc across the sky beyond the large windows, and all the vegetables stood prepared. He was cooking for Anya, and the roast needed at least three hours in a moderate oven to render it juicy and perfect. He opened the bottle of wine to breathe, a rare Malbec he had located at an exclusive wine boutique, and set it on the counter.

He wasn't much of a cook, but Jonah had explained what he wanted to do for Anya to his mom on a quick visit. She had jumped to the challenge, advising on food and wine; she'd even given Jonah a table-setting guide with pictures. The wine and food didn't matter to Jonah, but he wanted to impress Anya, and she clearly had much more experience than he did with the fancy things in life. It had taken a lot to explain Anya to his mom without including any details about The Realm, and he had ended his attempted explanation with, "Mom, she's the one, there's nothing more I can say..."

His mom had smiled and given him a tight hug. "I hope everything goes well, baby, this girl would be a fool to let you get away."

He'd walked away grinning. "You, mother dearest, are biased in your opinion."

Anya arrived at exactly six o'clock and rang his gate buzzer twice to let him know it was her. Jonah jogged from the living room, where he had left Diana Krall to croon softly on the sound system, to let her in. He stood fidgeting with a tiny white remote when she walked in, his back to the door, trying to get the music to play throughout the house. He turned to the door only once he got it working, and his jaw dropped at the sight of her.

She stood before him wearing a fitted deep red dress. He guessed it must be satin, the colour more like blood than wine. Her hair lay in large curls down her back and across her shoulders, to fall into her deep cleavage, and her makeup was old-Hollywood subtle and classy. He stood speechless, looking into her eyes.

"You take my breath away, you just..." Jonah eventually croaked, lowering the remote to a counter nearby.

Anya slowly lowered her eyes. "I wanted to look really nice tonight, it's been a difficult few weeks and I needed to do this, for me I think. Guess I want to feel pretty again."

Jonah strode up to her and kissed her cheek, breathing in her perfume and own unique smell as he rubbed his cheek against hers. He didn't lay a hand on her because he knew himself, as well as the strength of his desire for this woman.

"Anya, I cooked you dinner. Come, let's go get some. I apologise for walking you straight into food, but I need to occupy my hands or I'll do something I am bound to regret."

He never saw her satisfied little smile at the remark as he confirmed what Anya already knew, he still wanted her.

He led her into the kitchen and watched as she sniffed the air appreciatively. "That smells amazing, I haven't bothered to eat decently lately, there's been too much on my mind." She saw the wine and automatically reached for two glasses to pour it.

Every move she made accentuated her curves as the fabric of her dress slid over her skin, and Jonah felt so thoroughly on edge he could barely focus on removing the roast from the oven.

Every brush of hand past hand as they ate, or legs touching under the table, sent electric shocks through his skin and straight to his brain. Jonah felt as though he would die if he didn't have her right then and there, and

Anya felt exactly the same. As they finished eating, she glanced up furtively and met his gaze, and that was the moment which ended their evening of walking on eggshells around each other. She spoke just as he did.

"Jonah, I want…"

"Anya, I…"

They each instinctively knew that the other was about to say: 'I want you' and 'I need you'. They were the most obvious and cheesy sentiments, used in hundreds of books and movies, but right now, the only words needed. It was obvious, in the way Anya was dressed, in Jonah's efforts to make her dinner and impress her.

They stood simultaneously, mirrors of each other's movements as they leapt across the table between them. Neither heard the plates as they went crashing to the floor, or cared about the chair going flying as Anya threw it aside. Their lips met in a moment of perfection, with just the right amount of rough abandon, careless passion and deeply felt longing.

Anya clung to Jonah as he pulled her even tighter into his arms, gripping, yanking at fabric, his fingers tangling in her hair. Somewhere in the far distance they heard the tearing material, and Anya felt herself turned and pushed onto the edge of the table, sitting with her legs wrapped around Jonah's waist, her skirt in disarray around her.

Reality sunk for a moment through the thick fog of lust they were both drowning in, and Jonah held her face away from his, his lips still burning from the heat of their kiss.

"Are you sure you want this?" he asked, watching as her pupils focused on him.

Anya nodded. "More than anything, since the first night I met you, and especially since that one kiss…"

He let out a groan and lifted her into his arms.

"Bedroom," he muttered, walking toward the stairs.

As he went, Anya picked at the buttons of his shirt, undoing them one at a time. He carried her into his bedroom and placed her on the bed, then reached down to remove her shoes, tossing the stilettos toward the door. When she sat up he unzipped her dress, noticing the large tear down a side seam.

"I'm sorry about your…"

She cut him off with her lips on his, and pulled him onto the bed. "Forget the dress," she mumbled against his mouth. "You can always buy me another."

They tore at each other's clothes, and Jonah's buttons went flying as she ripped his shirt open the rest of the way. He threw her dress aside as she untangled the skirt from her legs, and when he sank down on top of her, their skin made contact, his chest against her breasts, his denim-clad legs entangled with her bare, smooth ones. While Jonah devoured Anya, kissing, nibbling and licking her neck, ears and décolletage, squeezing her firm breasts, she worked at his jeans, desperately trying to unbutton them.

Jonah raised himself off her body, sitting back on his knees to do the job she couldn't manage, and then stood to drop the jeans on the floor. Anya made little appreciative noises as she reached toward his erection, which strained at the fabric of his boxer briefs. He pushed her back onto the bed, pulling her toward the pillows and falling with renewed appetite on her breasts. While he bit and teased her nipples she moved against him, rubbing herself on his cock. Both of them still wore their underwear but Jonah felt the wetness and heat radiate from her sex as she moved.

Jonah reached for the bedside cabinet and a condom nearby, and then he lowered his body, crawling down the length of Anya's spread out form. He tugged her underwear down while she lay squirming and moaning beneath him, and he smiled as she raised her hips, allowing him to remove her underwear completely. This was surely the moment in a relationship every man lived for: the permission, the final 'okay' to go near a woman's most intimate body part.

Jonah tossed the scrap of fabric aside and lowered his mouth to the smooth, hairless lips as he pushed her legs farther apart. Tasting her was the most exquisite experience of Jonah's life, and he breathed deep the scent of her body. The heat of her skin scalded his lips as he licked her. Her fingers hesitantly, then firmly, tangled in his hair. He thought about why she might have hesitated and lifted his face.

"Anya, there is no Dominance or submission here tonight. We are simply a man and woman."

She nodded, and he kissed a path from her hipbones to her neck, using his one hand to balance and the other to remove his briefs. His cock bounced free to rub against her skin, and Anya moved more desperately against him, searching to instinctively guide him into her. He felt the urge to slip thoughtlessly into the comfort of her body, the sensation he'd longed for right there, but Jonah took a deep breath and lifted himself away from her.

Anya stroked his thigh while he rolled on the condom, and when he lowered himself to her again she claimed his lips, kissing him and exploring his mouth as he slid slowly and smoothly into her. She moaned softly against him and changed the angle of her hips to let him fill her completely. They froze, enjoying the feel of each other's bodies. Anya reached for Jonah's face and kissed him again and again while she held his face in her hands, then she started moving under him, relishing the little groans escaping his lips.

Jonah savoured the feel of her lips against his and her skin on his. He pulled Anya upright, and they adjusted their position so she sat on his lap, her hands on his thighs. Jonah placed his hand between them and with his thumb he kneaded her clit. He watched her face, her hair wild and plastered to her cheeks and neck. She had her eyes closed as she moved on him, and when his thumb made clit contact she dropped her head backward.

"Oh Jonah, oh God, don't stop that."

He dropped his gaze and saw her breasts moving as she did, the muscles of her flat stomach working under her smooth skin, her hairless sex against his hand. He gasped when he saw his cock as it slid in and out of her sex with his thrusts.

He increased his pressure, and she lifted her head, leaned close to kiss him as she uttered, "I am going to cum…"

The rest was lost in the convulsive tightening of her muscles around him, and her head fell forward onto his shoulder as she shuddered with release. Jonah breathed deeply as she moaned against his shoulder, and with his hands around her waist he lifted her off his cock to turn her around, placing her on her knees in front of him, her face buried in the pillows. When Jonah thrust into her again Anya clutched at the blankets and pillows, her knuckles turning white.

He pounded savagely into her, letting go of all the frustration and lust he'd felt for her over the past few months. He grabbed her hips and fucked her until she whimpered with the need to cum again, and when she did, he let his own orgasm wash over him. It was the most intense release he had ever experienced, and with his legs shaking and weakened, Jonah collapsed on top of Anya.

She giggled under him. "Guess you really like doggy style…" she mumbled from between the cushions.

Jonah rolled over onto his back. "Guess so." He playfully smacked her arse. "Apparently so do you."

Anya moved onto her side next to him and nodded, placing her hand on his chest. "I do."

They both took time to catch their breath and enjoy the comfortable sensation of being near another person. Anya was lonely in what she viewed as her new life, and not used to being alone. She knew she needed time to find herself again in the 'after Alex' phase, but that didn't make things any easier.

For Jonah, the moment was a point in his desire for Anya he had been dreaming about for a very long time. Having her in his bed was just the beginning, a step along the road from their first kiss.

***

They lay side by side on the destroyed bed-linen, basking in the afterglow one could only get from great sex.

Jonah exhaled. "So, anticipation eh?"

He chuckled when Anya playfully smacked his hand. She sat, scrambling to gather the pillows still left on the bed into a pile to lean against, and from her perch surveyed the mess around the bed. Linen and pillows were strewn far and wide, with a garnish of clothes sprinkled around.

She rubbed her eyes. "Geez, we made a hell of a mess."

As if to mock them and emphasize the truth in her statement, her stiletto fell over with a thud just inside the doorway.

When Anya sat back against her pile of pillows Jonah reached to stroke her leg. "Anya, I never fully understood the idea behind marking someone's skin until now, because fight the desire as I might, all I want to do is leave *my* marks all over you." He paused, and she saw him battle those urges; it showed in his eyes. "I have waited patiently to have you, through the destruction of both our relationships and the aftermath, and now that you're here, I don't want to share you, and if anyone else should see your skin I want them to know you are mine, only mine."

By the time Jonah finished speaking he sat in front of her on his knees, his head resting against her.

Anya was taken aback by his passionate statement because she had never suspected he had this side to him, and because she was scared of getting too involved too soon after her split with Alex. She took his hands in hers and frowned as she searched for the right words.

"Jonah, I want that, too, but not right this moment. I need a little time to think, time to breathe. Everything that's changed in my life has happened recently, and I'm not ready to walk from one Master/slave relationship into another." She was terrified of scaring him off, but had to be honest. "Can we spend a little time getting to know each other before we jump into anything involving marks and permanence?"

He nodded. "Of course, let's go and get some coffee and dessert in the meantime."

He pulled her up to her feet and they navigated the minefield of pillows and clothing with Anya following him down the stairs, through the dining room and into the kitchen. As they passed the table she bit her lip.

"Oh man, I'm sorry. There are broken plates and glasses."

Jonah shrugged. "Casualties of war, don't stress! I'll clean everything up tomorrow. Would you like to sleep over tonight? It makes sense, we might not be done yet…" He winked as he pulled coffee cups down from a shelf and switched on the Nespresso. "What time do you need to be at the office?"

Anya sank to the floor, sitting with her back to the cupboard. "Thanks, I would like to stay, if that's really okay. As for work, I only have appointments after lunchtime."

He brought coffee to her, passing the mug down before joining her on the floor. "I really meant that. I care for you

Anya, whether we take things slow or not. You are always welcome here."

They sat quietly enjoying the coffee, making small talk, until Jonah was startled from his lazy mood. "Crap! I forgot dessert!"

She put a hand on his arm when he tried to stand. "I don't want dessert, I am happy with coffee."

Jonah smiled at her. "Okay, tell me, where are you living now?"

He sat back again, cradling his mug while she spoke about life post-Alexander.

"I have a small room near my office, it's not much, but it will do for now." Misery rolled off her in waves.

"It can't be easy being confined after the life you got used to with Alex." He lifted his head. "Anya, I have a hell of a lot of space here, if you need to, why not move in here? I know you could probably do better, but I rattle through this old house like a ghost all alone, honestly, the presence of another human would be nice."

"Thanks Jonah, I will think about it. I do appreciate the offer, really," she said as she patted his leg.

They finished their coffee and walked back up the stairs. Anya paused in front of the large window overlooking the pool, staring wistfully at the water glimmering in the moonlight.

"Is it heated? The pool?" she asked, following Jonah the rest of the way.

"Yes. I haven't really spent any time in it, though."

Anya helped him tidy up the mess they'd left earlier and then jumped on the bed, curling up under the duvet, squirming around in the soft sheets. When Jonah joined her she snuggled close to him and murmured, "I can't believe I get to fall asleep beside you."

He stroked her hair. "I know, me too. I am glad you are here, thank you for staying with me."

After a moment's hesitation Jonah pulled her onto her back. "Listen, I need you to know that I don't want the type of relationship that you had with Alex. I want a girlfriend, and I want kinky sex, not a twenty four seven slave or submissive." He took a breath. "The Realm is great, don't get me wrong, but I don't think I am the kind of person who can handle the intensity of the lifestyle and rules everyone else seems to live by. And I thought about the marking skin desire, and when you want to wear my marks, you'll ask for them."

Anya smiled up at him in the dark. "Oh, will I, now? I like that idea for a relationship, it sounds… I want to say easy, it sounds normal, God knows I haven't had normal in forever." She curled up against him. "Let's talk more in the morning, or another time, when things aren't so fresh in our heads, or so raw."

***

When Anya woke up the next morning she was tightly cradled in Jonah's arms under the covers, and felt no desire to move, but her bladder thought differently. She carefully wiggled out from under his arm and scooted off the bed, padding to the bathroom to relieve herself.

After that, when she saw Jonah still sleeping soundly from the bathroom door, Anya made her way down to the dining room and kitchen, cleaned up the broken glass from the night before, stacked the dishwasher and started hunting coffee making goods. She tiptoed back to the bedroom, admiring the spacious passage and large rooms as she went, seriously thinking about Jonah's offer of living with him. Jonah was stretching as she entered the room again, and turned to smile at her.

"Now this I can seriously get used to."

She placed the coffee on his bedside table and sat down on the edge of the bed. "Nice isn't it? Service in bed?"

They drank their coffee and she looked at Jonah, comfortably reclined in the bed, pillows all around him. She felt that deep love stir inside her. Up to this point she had worked very hard to suppress what she felt for him, but she didn't think it was possible to keep it in much longer.

"Were you serious about me staying here?" She put her mug down and folded her hands on her lap.

Jonah nodded as he drank the coffee. "I am serious, you are more than welcome."

Anya thoughtfully stared into her own coffee. "Okay, I need a few days, but if you think you can live with me I'd like to take you up on that offer." She felt an inexplicable need to further explain herself. "You know, it's not that I can't afford anything, I just think it would be nice to be around another human, especially someone I actually like…"

Jonah stopped her rambling with a hand on her cheek. "Hush, it's okay. I understand. Take your time, and when you go home today I'll give you a set of keys so you can get in to come and go as you please. Okay?"

A single tear ran down her cheek when she looked up and met Jonah's gaze. "People are nothing but kind to me. You, Alex…" She sniffled and wiped at her cheek. "I don't deserve it. He saved my life, you know?" She looked at him with a bottomless well of hurt in her eyes.

Jonah sat upright and put his mug down to pull her into his arms. "Are you sure you did the right thing in leaving him? This much hurt can't be the result of a good choice."

She sat back. "I did the right thing, Jonah, I know I am going to hurt for a long time, and one day I'll tell you the story of how exactly he saved me, but it will get better, easier." She kissed him as the tears rolled down her cheeks. "I know, have known for a long time now, I belong with you."

The significance of those words was not lost on Jonah, and he felt his own eyes tear up as he dragged her back into bed. Tears mingled with laughter as they drowned in the fall of her hair over their faces and the covers being flung around them.

Chapter 11

Four weeks after the first time they had sex, Anya arrived home after a particularly hard day at work, and walked in to find him in the kitchen making coffee. "Pour the wine, I need a glass, badly." She kissed his cheek before sinking onto a chair.

Jonah reached for the bottle of Pinot Grigio in the refrigerator and poured a large glass for Anya.

"Want to talk?" he asked tentatively.

She shook her head and took a large sip. "Oh no, I absolutely don't want to talk, I have done enough talking for one day."

Jonah walked up behind her and rubbed her shoulders, pulling her suit jacket off and tossing it aside.

Anya moaned as he kneaded her tense muscles through the soft linen of her blouse, then she reached up and pulled his hands down to kiss them. "I do have a request though, if I may?" When she felt him nod behind her and make a little noise of approval, she leaned against him. "You remember saying I'd ask you?"

It felt so awkward, she had always been ordered to obey, but when Jonah froze she knew he'd understood and remembered what she was referring to.

She turned to face him. "This is me asking, no, begging for your marks. Please make me forget my own name for a while." She nuzzled his neck as she spoke.

From the position he was in behind her, instinct took over for Jonah. He didn't say a word but slid one hand into her hair and twisted it the soft strands using it as leverage as he pulled her to her feet. He half dragged, half walked her to the basement door where he stopped and raised her face to his to kiss her deeply, and hard.

Anya whimpered in his grasp and gooseflesh rose on the skin of her arms as Jonah held her face still and gazed into her eyes. He read excitement there, and just a touch of fear. She trembled as he looked at her in the silence of the house. He'd never thought seeing those two emotions in a woman's eyes would excite him so much.

Jonah released her, watching her stagger slightly in her heels.

"Go downstairs and lay out three implements, tools for me to mark your skin with, and stand under the chains to wait for me."

He turned away from her without any display of tenderness and walked back into the kitchen, where he picked up a pair of scissors, and fetched a bucket of ice from the large freezer. He stopped at the head of the stairs for a moment to calm his breathing. Jonah had managed not to show Anya how much this thrilled him, but he felt his heart race in his chest, and when he took that first step down he knew he was walking toward his future wife. Tonight he would mark her skin with his touch, and when he fucked her he would run his hands over the marks showing she was his, inexorably his.

***

The sound of Anya's breathing resonated through the basement, and as Jonah entered he dimmed the lights, watching her jump at the change. Her back was turned toward him, and Jonah ignored her as he tossed the scissors onto the massage table nearby and moved to place the ice bucket beside them. He kept all his movements measured and calm and by the time he came to stand behind her, he felt the calm he had faked until those moments finally settle in him.

Jonah ran his hands up and down her sides, over her clothing, and buried his face in her neck. "How long shall I make you forget your name for?" he murmured in her hair, squeezing her breasts in his hands as he spoke.

Anya leaned into him and let her head fall back on his shoulder. "I am yours, sir, to do with as you please for as long as you wish."

Jonah stepped away from her and walked toward the wall where his set of leather cuffs hung, lifted them off the hook and brought them to her, smiling when he saw the three implements she'd laid out: the crop, leather belt-strap and cane. He strapped the cuffs to her wrists and raised both arms to clip the attached carabiners to the chains, leaving her securely strung up and still fully dressed.

The clothing situation was soon to be rectified when he picked up the scissors from behind her and ran the edges over the fabric covering her breasts. Jonah smiled at her intake of breath and moved to stand behind her. He had no intention of uncovering her breasts tonight, and knelt down to slip the teeth of the scissors over the edge of her suit-skirt. Anya gasped as he cut her skirt all the way to the belt, rendering it irreparable and hanging only by the thin shred of fabric.

Jonah knew she liked the suit, and the destruction without protest was proof she submitted to his will. He was testing her reaction, and to him there was something obscene in destroying something so wantonly. Anya tried to move away when he ran the cold metal over her skin just above the line of her panties, but she was stuck in her position, stretched by the overhead cuffs. Jonah pulled the flimsy lace out of the way, to just below her arse, before he cut them off by snipping through the waistband at each hip. He wanted no fabric impeding his goals.

He dropped the panties to the floor after rubbing them between his fingers and feeling the obvious evidence of her arousal on them, smelling her feminine musk on the fabric. Then he tucked the remnants of her skirt to the sides of her hips.

The sight of her as he stood back to pick up the leather strap was a thing of beauty, as she hung there with her hair in disarray and lipstick smeared from his kiss, perfectly demure and covered from the front, from behind exposed and vulnerable. The pink and engorged lips of her sex hinted at her state from the cleft of her thighs as she arched her back. It took all of Jonah's self-control not to plunge into her welcoming body.

He held the strap in his hands and took a few steps to end up in front of her, the soles of his bare feet thudding on the rubber tiles. Jonah brushed the hair from Anya's face and lifted her chin.

"Before I do anything more, I want you to know you have safe words, okay? Just say orange if anything is worrying you or becoming too much and we can take a break. You say red, everything stops. Are we clear, baby?"

Anya nodded when he removed his hand from under her chin.

Jonah positioned himself behind her again, stroking the soft pale skin with the edge of the strap. "I don't want you to count or to thank me, not for these. Just feel and enjoy the knowledge that I am warming up your skin for the crop and cane." With one hand on her lower back Jonah raised the arm which held the strap and brought it down hard across her arse.

The crack of leather on skin reverberated through the space, stunning him. He'd never thought it could be so loud. Anya jerked on her restraints as he brought the heavy strap down again on the other cheek. Jonah ran a hand over the two thick red welts. He repeated the two strokes, overlapping them slightly with the first welts and weaving a subtle pattern on her skin. Jonah took his time, and when Anya gasped and cried out in pain with the tenth set of strokes, he laid the strap aside and went to stand in front of her again.

With one hand Jonah lifted her face to look into her eyes, wracked with pain and showing endurance. She bit her lip as he kissed her forehead.

"You are going to take more for me, aren't you, Anya?" Jonah whispered, the soft sound alien in the large room after the noise of the strap.

Anya nodded, even while tears ran down her cheeks. Jonah reached around her and cupped her burning arse in his palms, squeezing the heated skin and smiling as she bit back a cry. He patted her cheek softly, a little put-off when she flinched from the gesture.

"I will never slap you in the face Anya, I don't want you ever flinching from my touch to your face, okay?"

She nodded.

"Good girl." He picked up the crop and flicked it through the air. "Hmm, this is going to leave some pretty patterns over those welts," he murmured cheerfully, and brought the head of the crop down hard on the back of her thigh.

Anya let out a scream and lifted her foot to get the thigh out of his aim from another smack. Jonah simply placed it on the other leg. He watched as she skipped from foot to foot yelping and squealing, her shoes falling off and her position becoming more strained without the height of heels. Jonah kicked her shoes out of the way and chuckled as he placed small and precise marks down the backs of her thighs, stopping when she shook her head violently, shouting, "Stop! Please stop, I can't breathe. Oh God, that hurts!"

From behind her, Jonah yanked her head back with his fingers twisted in her hair. "If you can't handle this, how on earth will you manage the cane?" He grunted the words in her ear. He was lost to himself, completely absorbed in the moment, and while he spoke, he laid a series of short and rapid blows down her one thigh, and then switched sides, until Anya yelled, "Orange!"

He stopped and tossed the crop aside.

She hung gasping in the restraints, hair plastered to her face with sweat and tears soaking her face down to the collar of her shirt. She opened her eyes and looked into his, and Jonah lowered his mouth to hers, pushing past the boundary of her lips to probe the depths of her mouth with his tongue. He kissed her possessively as she mewled softly against his mouth, and when he released her she hung limp in the cuffs.

Jonah reached up and unhooked the cuffs from the chains, seeing her fingers turn a bad shade of blue from lack of blood, and bent her forward over the massage table. This was a much better position for the cane, he thought. When he picked up the cane he walked around and knelt beside where her head lay, her eyes mildly panicked as she saw it in his hands.

"No, please no..." she whimpered softly, hiding behind her hair at the sight.

He wiped the fall of hair from her face and whispered in her ear, "That's not your safe word, Anya, do you want to use the safe word?" He stroked her back and saw her relax under his touch.

She took a deep breath before replying, "No sir." She closed her eyes.

"Good girl," he said as he stood and walked behind her, kicking her feet wider apart and folding her tattered skirt out of the way. He ran the tip of the cane over her already red and hot cheeks. Jonah saw the wide space beside her and lifted the cane, bringing it down with a thud on the bed beside her. Anya jumped and stared wide-eyed at the cane in front of her face as he lifted it away again.

She lifted her head to shake it again, over and over, mouthing the word 'no' as she did, and when the first stroke landed on her, she froze, every muscle in her body stiffening. It seemed to take a while for the nerves to comprehend the pain, and as he watched, her toes curled.

"You're going to take ten of those for me Anya."

Jonah laid another, and then a third stroke parallel. She was twisting and convulsing to try and avoid them, and he moved to hold her with a hand on the small of her back, pushing down on her as she struggled to catch her breath. He didn't let her body get used to any rhythm; he kept going until he reached his goal of ten strokes. When he got to ten Jonah dropped the cane near the crop and ran his nails over the tiger stripes on her arse. Mingled with the belt welts and crop marks they formed a piece of art.

Anya moaned softly against him and lifted her head to turn it toward him. "Is that ten?" she asked carefully, and he nodded.

She smiled. "Oh thank fuck. No more, please, I can't."

Jonah leaned over her, his jeans rubbing against the raw skin. "What's your name?" he asked with a chuckle, and she burst into giggles.

"Hmph…" she muttered unintelligibly against the bed, as her hands curled into fists beside her face.

Jonah wiped her hair aside. "Now, I am going to fuck you." He reached for his buckle to undo his jeans as the euphoric rush of what they had just done took a hold.

While he leaned against her, he freed his cock, which had been achingly erect since he laid the first cane stripe on her, and slid in one smooth movement into her soaking wet sex. Anya cried out under him, and Jonah saw stars, the sensation of their bodies skin on skin was so intense.

"Your pussy is so needy right now, perfectly ready for me after having your arse abused," he murmured against her. He grasped her waist and raised himself to thrust roughly into her, and felt her sex tighten around him as she shook and trembled with her orgasm.

Jonah realised this was it, he was inside her and there were no barriers. They had both gone for standard STI tests shortly after she moved in, but he had been waiting for a special moment to do this. He stopped his movement, buried to the hilt in her, and coated in the liquid of their fucking.

"Anya, I am going to cum inside you tonight, fill you with my essence. You are mine after this, no other man will ever lay their hands on you again."

He growled in her ear as she hollowed her back under him and replied, "I am yours, as you are mine, and have been for a while now, but this..." She pulled one of his hands to where she could kiss it.

With those words Jonah let go and emptied himself into her body.

"Mine, only mine," he mouthed in her ear a last time.

***

After they'd both regained their senses and Jonah had carried Anya to their bedroom, he stood her up in the bathroom to remove the rest of her clothing, admiring the marks on her arse and thighs. There were welts from the heavy belt strap, stripes from the cane as well as small oval bruises from the crop.

"I think I did a fairly thorough job, for a first timer." He turned her, to show her in the mirror.

Anya exhaled and ran a hand through her hair, pulling it into a rough bun on top of her head. "I'd say."

Her skin stood red, welted and bruised from the top of her arse to the backs of her knees, and Jonah couldn't have been happier. He frowned. "I am confused about why this sight makes me so happy. Seeing you so marked and bruised." He walked her into the bathroom and turned on taps to run hot water into the large tub.

She sighed. "I am happy too. It's just a more primal way of showing ownership, Jonah, let it be, and enjoy it without worrying. Liking this doesn't make you a bad person, it's consensual and enjoyed by me, too."

He pulled her into his arms. "I love you, thank you for everything you've given me, Anya."

As they stood engrossed in each other, the bath overflowed, but neither of them could be swayed from the object of their affection, the only other person in the room. The world vanished, and being held and holding was the only thing they cared about at that moment in time.

***

The weekend following the night in Jonah's dungeon, there was a function to attend at The Realm, and Jonah stood with his hands in his pockets watching Anya as she dressed early in the evening. Her sapphire blue dress clung to every curve and accentuated the colour of her eyes. Heels graced her petite feet, and raised her to almost his height.

"It will be nice to see people more formally dressed, instead of naked," Jonah said with relief, and she nodded, applying lipstick.

They were attending a cocktail party for members and non-members, a marketing gimmick for the club itself, to be used by the vanilla community on nights when it usually stood dark and dormant. It was a way for Realm members to meet new people, and a way of generating revenue for the business. Since the accident Alex had never let slip any details; the club had undergone a total makeover. Alex had refurbished the outside of the building, as well as making the inside a lot more non-kink friendly, with hidden doors and concealed staircases. Security was ramped up, and easily accessible parking was built for non-members.

There were also two new managers, one for BDSM events, and one for normal club nights: dancing, drinking and the things people normally got up to. The normal manager had been informed of BDSM activities, but was kept in the dark about The Realm. Jonah had watched Alex slowly withdraw from the social world, his presence more often than not lacking, and he knew something was up. The split from Anya had done something terrible to him, and left him broken.

It had been almost a year since Jonah had been initiated, and he enjoyed doing the accounting for the club. He marvelled on an almost constant basis at how much both he and his life had changed since that first terrifying night.

Anya walked up to him and kissed his cheek. "Shall we go? I don't think we should be late."

They drove in silence with Diana Krall playing in the background, singing 'Let's fall in love…'

Jonah smiled secretively, patting the pocket of his suit jacket to feel the ring box, snug, there.

Epilogue

Light and jazzy music played throughout the venue. Waiters, the slaves who usually wafted around in sheer garments and collars, walked gracefully between patrons holding trays of champagne and canapes. This evening they were dressed in slinky, black satin cocktail dresses and no collars were present. Instead, each wore a delicate silver ankle chain with an ornate padlock.

Jonah guided Anya to a spot on the dance floor and they swayed to the music, bodies pressing in on them from all around. He kissed her neck as she placed her head beside his.

"It's so busy!" Anya said, bumped from behind by a boisterous young lady who immediately turned to apologise with a loud, "Sorry!"

Tonight was special for Jonah, and for Anya, he hoped. He had arranged a key for the basement dungeon, and now led Anya toward the newly concealed entrance to it. She frowned.

"Where are we going, Jonah?" she asked suspiciously.

He smiled as he turned to her. "Just trust me okay? Come!"

Candles burned all the way down the stairs and in the stone circle on the floor. She stared around her as he positioned her in the middle of the circle of light.

"Anya, I brought you here because this is where my life was forever changed." Jonah stared around as he spoke and moved to pick up the silver chalice from a ceremonial table nearby. It was then Anya noticed Bartholomew in the shadows and curtsied to him politely. He merely inclined his head toward her with a slight smile in response.

Anya felt her panic rise as Jonah approached with the chalice, and produced a small dagger from his pocket. She recognised it as the ritual dagger of The Realm, used at initiations and collaring ceremonies, and her stomach twisted into knots as she watched Jonah prick his palm, allowing a few drops of his blood to run onto the silver, polished blade.

"I entered this basement as a stranger to myself and walked out into the world as a new man." He stirred the blood into the chalice of wine, and she knew with certainty what he was going to ask. Claustrophobia overwhelmed her and she almost sank to her knees, but he reached for her shaking hand and supported her.

"It has been almost a year since I was last down here, and this time is different." He set the chalice back on the table and took both her hands in his. "Anya, I don't want a slave or submissive in you, I don't want to put a collar around your neck and claim ownership. I want a life partner, someone equal to me, who chooses to enjoy the darker side of my needs and urges, as I do."

He released one hand to reach into his suit pocket, and when he brought the hand out, he knelt in front of her. Tears filled Anya's eyes and she clasped her hands over her mouth as he opened the box to reveal a shining diamond ring.

"Anya, will you be my wife, my equal, my partner, a lover who chooses to be, at times submissive and subservient, but always equal? Will you be the mother of my children? Share my life, please."

He gazed at her with eyes so full of love she could only nod and try to mouth the word 'yes' incoherently through her tears. He smiled broadly and took the ring from the box to slip it onto her finger. When she looked down she noticed it was an intricate design, like a knotted rope studded with diamonds, set in Celtic knots.

Next, Jonah picked up the chalice and held it to her. "Bind yourself to me in every possible way, then, and drink of my blood."

He handed it to her and watched as she sipped, then downed the contents before replying, "I am yours and you are in me, always."

Bartholomew approached them and laid a hand on each's shoulder. Kissing their cheeks one at a time he pronounced, "It is done, you are free of your bond to Alex. You two are now tied to each other."

Jonah pulled Anya into his arms and kissed her passionately. Pulling away from her after a moment, he said, "Now we can begin our lives together."

She smiled. Anya felt a mixture of regret for the pain Alex would feel, and ecstasy at the promise of the future.

She tried to hide her emotions and caught Bartholomew's head-shake as he left the chamber.

"What have we been doing up until now?" she asked, focusing her attention on Jonah.

He raised an eyebrow. "We have been writing the introduction to our story."

He lifted her in his arms and spun her around as she giggled.

***

On the main floor Alex felt the disconnect as Anya severed her bond to him by drinking Jonah's blood in her wine. It was a painful sensation, and he felt for a moment sick to his stomach, and doubled over. It was the last thing he had anticipated, even though he'd known it was coming, and he slammed his glass down on the counter to run from the room. He had been denying this to himself, always silently hoping Anya would come home to him. He ignored the stares of patrons and members of The Realm alike as he moved through the crowds.

He strode straight out of the club right then, without saying goodbye to a single person, and stood for a long time in the road. After a deep breath and loud exhale he climbed onto his bike, revved the engine and sped off into the dark. Alex had no idea where he was going, or how he would get there, but he needed to get away from her, from them, from his entire life. He had his passport and wallet in his pocket, and nothing else.

Alex only stopped once he got to the airport, and using internet banking, he cleared all but one of his accounts. He bought new clothing, dropped his suit in the trash, and walked straight to the Emirates flight counter.

"One ticket on your next flight to Dubai, please."

The clarity that he needed to start a new life elsewhere hit him like a brick as he said this. It was not a temporary escape he had anticipated. Instead he knew that he'd be running from his own feelings forever.

Nobody ever saw him again in the United States, and his letter with the instructions for wrapping up his business was found the next morning, by the cleaning staff at the club.